Dear Readers,

With Valentine's Day right around the corner, it's a red-letter month for love, and Bouquet is delivering the right romances to put you in the mood!

Legendary Zebra author Colleen Faulkner starts us off this month with **Maggie's Baby,** the story of one woman's painful loss—and her emotional reunion with the only man who can change her past mistakes into a future that holds the promise of love. **Cookies and Kisses,** from Gina Jackson, tackles the lighter side of love with this sweet story of a man who decides his wholesome neighbor would make a great weapon in his custody battle—until he develops "forever" kind of feelings for his temporary wife.

Sometimes love is found in the most unlikely places. In longtime Harlequin author Vanessa Grant's **The Colors of Love,** a sensible physician believes that the free-spirited artist he meets by chance is the wrong woman for him—until she convinces him that their attraction is not only red-hot, but true blue. Finally, Jove and Zebra author Ann Josephson offers **Coming Home,** the story of a successful businessman returning to his rural hometown, searching for a simpler life—but finding the beautiful owner of a local quilt shop is an attractive complication.

A dozen red roses, a box of candy . . . and four fantastic, brand-new Bouquet romances—what better way to celebrate the only day devoted to love?

Kate Duffy
Editorial Director

FIRST LOVE

Jarrett tried to collect his thoughts. Over the years he'd planned what he would do, what he would say, if Maggie ever showed up on his doorstep. But when he'd rehearsed, he hadn't taken into account the feelings that would accompany her arrival.

Seeing Maggie like this after all these years had brought a flood of emotions he didn't want to deal with right now—ever, if he could help it. He had expected to be angry with her. What he hadn't expected was the strange tightening in his chest that was something akin to want, need. He experienced a sense of loss he hadn't felt in a long time. A sense of longing.

No woman had ever touched his heart the way Maggie had, not in all these years . . .

MAGGIE'S BABY

COLLEEN FAULKNER

Zebra Books
Kensington Publishing Corp.

http://www.zebrabooks.com

ZEBRA BOOKS are published by

Kensington Publishing Corp.
850 Third Avenue
New York, NY 10022

Zebra and the Z logo Reg. U.S. Pat. & TM Off.

First Printing: February, 2000
10 9 8 7 6 5 4 3 2 1

Printed in the United States of America

This one's for you Mary—
a contemporary at last!

PROLOGUE

Talbany General Hospital
Talbany Beach, Delaware
The Present

Dr. Maggie Turner walked down the brightly lit hospital corridor and dug into the pocket of her white lab coat for the half-eaten candy bar she knew was in there. She pulled out a pen, alcohol wipes, a sealed syringe, and a rubber glove before she found the candy.

A broken femur had kept her from the dark chocolate confection. Another foolish college kid—too much to drink, a balcony on his parents' half-million-dollar third-story condo. She knew the scenario all too well. The little jackass had a blood alcohol level of .15. The boy who rode in the ambulance with the kid said his friend had claimed he could fly. He was lucky he hadn't broken his neck and wound up a paraplegic in a wheelchair. Damned lucky.

Maggie bit into her rich chocolate dinner. She'd wash it down with the flat Diet Pepsi she'd left in the physician's lounge.

"Maggie." Dr. Jeb Marshal glanced up as he passed her, his Mont Blanc pen poised.

"Jeb." She nodded cordially. He was a geeky kind of guy, all with long arms and legs. But he was pleasant enough and he kept his hands off her in the surgical room, which was more than she could say for many of her male colleagues. Besides, he was one hell of a cardiologist.

"Slow night?" he asked, glancing over the frames of his tortoiseshell glasses.

She raised one shoulder. "The MI you saw, an ear infection, two sunburns, and a balcony flier." She nodded, satisfied. "Very slow night."

"Just wait. The full moon is coming." He raised an eyebrow, Groucho Marx style.

Maggie laughed, but made no further comment. Jeb turned at the end of the hallway and disappeared.

She smiled to herself as she passed exam room four, headed for the physician's lounge. Jeb had a bad crush on her. All the nurses in the ER were twittering about it.

Of course, Maggie wasn't interested. She was married, for God's sake—a wife and a mother.

Thoughts of three-year-old Jordan and his chubby cheeks made Maggie smile again. She hadn't seen him all week and she had a long weekend coming up, the first in months. Little Jordan and her husband were coming from DC to stay in their beach house.

It was a pain in the ass, this commuter marriage, but it worked for her and Stanley. There had been no decent job offers in the DC area, and Talbany General had offered her an excellent position in the ER and interest-free loans to pay what she still owed for med school. Maggie certainly couldn't have asked Stanley to leave his job and move to the shore, and Stanley hadn't offered.

Actually, if Maggie allowed herself to admit it, she missed Jordan more than she did her husband.

She ate the last square of chocolate and crumbled the wrapper in the palm of her hand. She wasn't ready to admit her marriage was a failure, doomed from the start. She wasn't ready to give up. *It's the distance between us,* she kept telling herself. *His business. My job here in the ER with its twelve-hour shifts. Having a toddler and two full-time jobs is enough to make anyone's relationship rocky.*

Maggie tossed the candy wrapper in the garbage can behind the registration desk from the foul line taped on the floor for an easy basket.

"Good shot, Dr. Turner. We could use you on the staff team. Carney's Body Shop tore us up in the semis." One of the orderlies passed her, carrying a suture tray—probably for her flier, who had a scalp laceration over his eyebrow. Maggie had left Jason, a physician's assistant, to do the sutures. He needed the practice.

"Thanks."

"Dr. Turner, Dr. Turner, line one please," came a mechanical female voice over the intercom.

Maggie picked up the nearest wall phone and punched the switchboard line, wondering if that same unemotional voice worked the intercom in every hospital in the free world. She was certain it was the same voice she'd heard at Hahnemann every day and night of her residency. "Dr. Turner."

"Please hold."

There was a click, followed by another. Then static.

"Stanley?" It had to be Stanley on his cellular car phone. The interference was always bad.

"Maggie?" More static.

"Hi, Stanley." She leaned against the white wall, staring at the green stripe on the floor that led patients toward the labs. A young woman in blue overalls was busy mopping the green line, the antiseptic smell of her detergent wafting down the hallway. Maggie turned her back to the cleaning lady, selfishly not wanting to share her phone call. "How's Jordan?"

"Good. Just picked him up from day care. We're going out for dinner. Meeting a friend." The phone line crackled. "—wanted to tell you we'll be in late Friday night."

"OK. Can I speak to Jordan for a minute?"

"Here he is."

She strained to hear. "Jordan?"

"Mommy?"

Maggie broke into a warm smile. "Hi there, pumpkin. How was Miss Jean's today?"

"Good, Mommy," his sweet voice came over the static. "I drew dinner-saur today. Jessie ate my jelly sam-which."

"Oh, no! Tell me, was it a big dinosaur you drew?"

The static eased off and she could hear his voice clearly, a voice that no longer sounded so babyish to her. He was growing up quickly, too quickly. "T rex."

"I bet you did a great job."

Jordan was fascinated with dinosaurs. During their last long weekend together, she and Stanley had taken him to the Museum of Natural History in DC to see the dinosaur bones.

"With purple teeth," added the toddler.

"Wow." Maggie's eyes widened. "Well, Mommy has to go."

"To fix sick peoples?"

The static was beginning again. "That's right," Maggie said. "To fix sick people. Now you save the picture for my refrigerator. Daddy's bringing you to the beach this weekend." She paused. "I really miss you, Jordan."

"Miss you, Mommy."

Maggie's throat constricted. "Jordan, I love—"

"Sorry. He's gone," came Stanley's voice. "Power Rangers win again."

"Put him back on." Again came the crackling sound of static over the phone line as the signal came and went. "I want to tell him I love him."

"What? Sorry. Can't hear you, Mags. Bad connection." The crackling filled her ear. "Got to go. See you Friday night."

The phone clicked and the connection was broken.

Maggie gripped the receiver. She considered calling back. She wanted to tell Jordan she loved him. She never got to tell him often enough these days.

But she hung up the phone, feeling silly for her sudden wave of emotion. It had to be PMS. She'd just wait and tell Jordan she loved him in person on Friday. It was only two days away.

"Dr. Turner."

Maggie looked up to see the charge nurse in a

yellow-flowered smock rush by. "Got two near drownings coming in. Jet ski accident on the bay."

"More college kids?"

She nodded. "Who else?"

Maggie sighed, falling into step behind her. Heaven help them. It was only June. It was going to be a long summer.

For the next two hours, Maggie worked on the two jet ski accident patients. One was finally admitted with a skull fracture and a punctured lung. The luckier one was sent home with abrasions and contusions and one arm in a cast.

Tossing her green disposable gown into the garbage as she exited trauma one, Maggie headed for the physician's lounge, determined to get a sip of the Diet Pepsi she'd opened hours before. She checked her Timex. It was nearly ten p.m. The drunks would start rolling in, in another hour or so.

She pushed through the door of the physician's lounge. The room, decorated in early Salvation Army, was empty. It smelled of coffee, stale donuts, and sleepless nights. A half-eaten pastrami on rye sat in its waxed paper wrapper beside an abandoned bottle of apple juice. There were piles of newspapers and magazines everywhere. The cushions of the worn couch were still indented from the last fatigued occupant.

She heard the perk of the coffeemaker and smelled its contents as thick, dark brew spurted like an arterial vein into the glass pot on a table near the phone. At least someone had had the decency to start a fresh pot. Coffee was the lifeblood of night-shift ER physicians and nurses.

Maggie crossed the worn green carpet and opened the fridge in search of her soda. She pushed aside half of a cantaloupe. There it was, with her name penned over the red, white, and blue logo as if she were still in nursery school. She guessed some things never changed. She closed the door and leaned against it as she took a sip. The soda had lost its fizz, but at least it was cold.

"Dr. Turner?"

Maggie looked up to see a six-foot-five state trooper removing his Smokey the Bear hat. The lounge door swung shut behind him. The young man looked as if he was barely out of the academy. His clean-shaven face was pale.

"What can I do for you, trooper?" She took another sip of the diet soda, still leaning casually against the refrigerator. In her line of work, she dealt with the police often.

He exhaled and looked away, and she realized his eyes were filling with tears.

Maggie lowered the can from her lips and glanced at the name badge on his pressed uniform shirt. Something was wrong, terribly wrong. An icy trickle of fear ran down her spine. "Trooper Eames?"

The trooper looked back at her, seeming to gather his wits. "Dr. Maggie Turner?"

She nodded and approached him, suddenly feeling as if she were moving in slow motion. For some reason, she had an immediate and desperate need to cover his mouth, to keep him from speaking.

"I'm so sorry, Dr. Turner, but there's been an accident on the DC beltway . . ."

Maggie heard the mechanical intercom voice. Someone had called a code blue. CCU. Second floor.

Maggie shook her head. The Pepsi can slipped from her fingers. She heard it hit the floor, felt the splash against her khakis. She was still walking toward the trooper, but it was taking so damned long to get to him. His words were still tumbling out, words she'd spoken herself to victims' families.

"Your husband and son—"

Maggie shook her head. "No," she whispered. "I just spoke to them on the phone not two hours ago. Jordan drew a T rex."

"The EMTs did all they could, doctor." Tears were now running down the trooper's broad cheeks. "I'm so sorry."

"No," Maggie said. Her voice was firm, but already numbness was washing over her—a numbness she recognized all too well. "No, not my Jordan. Not my little boy. You've made a mistake."

"I'm afraid not, doctor. They were dead on arrival at the city hospital. Your sister," he glanced at a slip of paper in his hand, "a Mrs. Lisa Jones, already identified the bodies." He looked up at Maggie. "I'm supposed to take you there. Is there someone I can call to ride with you?"

Maggie fell to her knees on the stained green carpet, clasping her hands in prayer. "No," she begged. "Not my baby." She bowed her head, hot tears streaming down her face. Her heart was breaking; she could feel the agony as scarred flesh and muscle tore. Suddenly the past came screaming back, jumbling with the pre-

sent until there was no difference between this child
and the last.

"Not my baby," she repeated. "Dear God, not
again . . ."

ONE

June, 1983

"Not again." Seventeen-year-old Maggie Turner stood in front of the cracked mirror of her dresser, her head upside down as she brushed out her reddish-blond hair. "I just talked to him twenty minutes ago."

Maggie's mother, Ruth, stood in the doorway, the phone in her hand, the cord stretched taut from the kitchen. She covered the receiver with her hand; a non-filter cigarette dangled from the corner of her mouth. "If the McKay boy wants to talk to you, you take the phone."

Maggie rolled her eyes as she raised her head and flung her hair over her back. Ruth Turner was obsessed with the McKay family—with any family in Belltown, for that matter, who had a house with a pool and an automatic lawn sprinkler system. She encouraged her daughter to make friends with the girls from wealthy families, encouraged her to date their brothers. She insisted Maggie take golf, tennis, and horseback riding lessons so she would "fit in."

Maggie sighed, grabbed a rubber band from a

cracked dish of barrettes on her dresser, and pulled her mane of hair back into a ponytail. Of course, secretly she was pleased Jarrett McKay was calling her three times a day. Pleased, heck. She was ecstatic! Now if he'd only ask her out.

Maggie took the phone from her mother's hand, then gave her a "back off" stare. Ruth threw up her hands in surrender and retreated down the hallway in her yellowed nurse's aide uniform, a cloud of cigarette smoke billowing behind her. She worked the swing shift at the local old folks' home. She also moonlighted, sitting with elderly patients in their private rooms at night. The good thing about the job was that Maggie and her sister Lisa had free rein in the evenings to come and go as they pleased. As long as they didn't disturb their father, who was usually asleep in his chair in front of the TV, no one was there to hand out ultimatums or assign chores.

Maggie ducked into the bathroom and closed the door behind her, then dropped the lid on the john and sat down on the faded orange cover. "Jarrett? What's up? I just talked to you a few minutes ago." She caught a piece of her ponytail and wound it around her finger. She was so nervous she could barely keep her voice steady.

"I know, but now I'm calling back because—" His voice was warm and sexy.

"Because?" Maggie held her breath. This was it. This was what she'd been waiting for. He was older than Maggie and had just finished his freshman year at

Georgetown University. Maggie would be going into her senior year in high school in September.

"Because why?" Maggie repeated, barely able to contain herself. It was so hard to act cool about this whole dating thing when she'd had so few dates. Her mother was so particular about whom she hung around with that she'd had very little chance to date at all.

"Only the best for my daughter," Ruth Turner had said again and again as she turned down one would-be suitor after another. Joey Matuchi's parents owned a meat market. "You'll spend your life stinking of fish," Ruth had said. Jerry McDonald's father was a town cop. "Late nights and piss-poor pay." Ruth Turner was determined her daughter wouldn't end up in a thousand-square-foot, two-bedroom bungalow and taking a second job to pay the taxes.

"I called you back because I just got my birthday present from my parents," Jarrett said.

"I didn't know it was your birthday." She brushed her forehead with her hand. It was so hot in their house. Maggie and her sister had been begging for a room air conditioner for weeks, but Ruth said they couldn't afford it. "Nineteen, wow. An old geezer. Why didn't you tell me?"

"Ah, I don't know. I'm not into birthdays. But anyway, listen—you'll never believe this. My dad got me a car!"

"A car!" Maggie jumped up. "You said they said you couldn't have one. Something about earning your way in the world."

"They wanted to surprise me." His excitement came

over the phone line. "And, Maggie, it is such a cool car. Wait till you see it!"

"What is it?"

"A '68 Ford Mustang convertible."

Maggie squealed. "Red?"

"Cherry."

She squealed again. "Oh, wow, Jarrett. Did you drive it yet?"

"Just around the block. My old man wanted to go over the *safety features.*"

"And how was it? The ride, not the *safety features.*" She laughed with him at her own joke.

"Better than I thought it would be." There was pause on Jarrett's end of the phone line. "I really wanted you to go with me to test drive her. That's why I waited. I thought we'd cruise for a while and then get pizza at Tony's."

Maggie glanced in the bathroom mirror. She couldn't go on a date looking like this. She didn't have a lick of mascara on her lashes and her hair was limp from the humidity. She'd been cleaning out the refrigerator, for heaven's sake.

"So do you think you could go?"

Maggie stared at the face from hell in the mirror. "Sure. Sounds like fun."

"Your parents will let you go?"

She shrugged, already yanking the rubber band from her hair. Maybe her sister would let her borrow her hot curlers. Better yet, maybe Lisa wasn't home and Maggie could borrow them without having to beg and plead. "My mom's volunteering." That was what she was instructed to say when Ruth was working, because mothers from well-to-do families didn't work. "And Dad doesn't care as long as I'm in by eleven." That was usually when he woke up long enough to walk from his recliner to his bed.

"Great. I'll pick you up in an hour."

She ran her fingers through her hair, knowing it was going to be impossible to do anything with it on a hot afternoon like his. "Sure."

He paused again. Maggie waited.

Finally Jarrett's amused voice came across the line again. "Maggie, you have to tell me where you live if I'm going to pick you up."

She laughed, hesitating for only an instant. "107 Ivy Drive. I'll be out front."

"Great. See you."

Maggie leaned against the bathroom door, savoring the moment. Jarrett McKay had asked her out. This was it. Finally her life was going to begin. "See you."

The moment Maggie stepped out of the bathroom, Ruth followed her down the hallway to the kitchen. "So what did the McKay boy want?"

"His name is Jarrett, Mother." She hung up the phone on the wall next to the back door. "And he asked me out."

"Finally." Ruth turned and followed her daughter back down he hallway covered by green indoor-outdoor carpet. "Where's he taking you? Swimming at the county club?"

"We're just going for a ride, Mother. That and

pizza." Maggie tried to sound nonchalant. "No big deal."

"No big deal? Thank God I took that second mortgage out to pay for your braces. This is the opportunity we've been waiting for."

Maggie stopped at the door of the bedroom she shared with her sister. "No, it's the opportunity *you've* been waiting for, Mother. I just like him. He's nice. Not like the other guys."

"He's going to Georgetown University, Maggie. They say prelaw."

Her mother was always full of "they says," but Maggie could never figure out just who *they* were. "Jarrett's uncle is a lawyer. Everyone in his family's pushing him to go into law, too, but he doesn't know what he wants to do. He's taking business classes for now."

Ruth stood in the hall, her cigarette dangling from the lipstick-smudged corner of her mouth. "Well, you behave. Be polite. If he asks you to go home with him, you go. Meet his parents. You establish yourself right away. Once you meet some of his friends, you'll be free to move on."

Maggie looked away, embarrassed by her mother's litany. "I've got to get ready, Mom. Have a good night at work. I hope Mr. Jansen stays in his bed." She ducked into her bedroom.

"Maggie? Where did you say you lived?"

Maggie stuck her head back through the doorway and sighed. She felt guilty for the deceit, but it was the only way her mother would let her go out. "Ivy Drive."

"Good. You keep it that way." Then Ruth was gone

and Maggie was left to get ready for her first date with Jarrett in peace.

Forty-five minutes later, Maggie hurried down the sidewalk, her satchel purse slung over her shoulder. Shoot, she was going to be covered with sweat by the time she reached the house. She'd just die if Jarrett pulled up and her pits were wet. She flapped her arms as she walked, hoping the summer breeze would keep her underarms dry.

She'd dressed carefully for her first date with Jarrett, changing three times. She wanted him to think she was fun, but that she was no Lisa. Finally she'd decided on denim shorts and a sleeveless white blouse that buttoned up the front. Casual, but classy. "Dress like your daddy's got a million, even if he hasn't," Ruth's voice buzzed in her head.

Maggie had used Lisa's hot curlers and done a half-decent job with her hair, wearing it long down her back, pulled back at the crown of her head with a leather barrette. Sexy, but sophisticated.

Ahead and across the street, she spotted the house at 107 Ivy Drive. It was a two-story brick Colonial with a two-car garage and a lawn sprinkler system that went off like clockwork at seven a.m. every summer morning.

Years ago Ruth Turner had picked this house, two neighborhoods over, as their established residence. Mail came to a PO box in town, but this was where the Turners officially lived—or at least pretended to live.

Maggie had thought her mother was crazy that August day in the summer of her sixth-grade year when they'd moved from the trailer park in Exton to Bell-town. That was really when her mother's obsession with the Belltown elite had begun. Ruth had crammed Maggie's belongings into the trunk, Barbie dolls and all, leaving Lisa at the trailer to help her father load everything else into a borrowed bread truck.

Ruth had driven Maggie directly to the house on Ivy Drive and parked their rusty Impala across the street from the brick colonial. Maggie instantly fell in love with the house and the neighborhood. Here the air had smelled of fresh cut grass and steaks cooking on a grill. Maggie had never had a steak cooked on a grill, but she could just imagine what it would taste like from the heavenly scent in the air. There were no junked cars, or yard sale leftovers thrown in the street, no weeds in the manicured lawn.

"There she is. Isn't she beautiful?" Ruth smiled, a rare occasion.

"We bought this house?" Maggie breathed. It was the mos, beautiful house she had ever seen in her life, prettier than a dollhouse in the Sears catalog. On the side porch, a swing glided in the breeze.

Ruth ground her butt in the ashtray and reached for another cigarette in the same motion. "Where do you think I'd get the money for a damned mansion like this? Certainly not from The Bread Man." That was what she called Maggie's dad. Not honey, not sweetheart, not even Bob. The Bread Man.

Maggie sagged in her seat. Of course she hadn't believed she was going to live in a brick house with a white picket fence and flowers in the window boxes.

She was too old to believe in fairy tales. But it had been fun to think so, if only for a few seconds.

Maggie stared at the worn sneakers on her feet. "So why did you bring me here?"

"Because I told the school this is where we live."

Maggie stared at her mother, whose short-cropped helmet of streaked hair and bright peach lipstick had gone out of fashion years ago. "I don't understand."

"Our new house is a couple streets over. The cheap neighborhood, Maggie. This," she pointed, "is the house we're gonna *say* we live in." Ruth blew smoke in exasperation. "The school will think you live here. The bus will pick you up on this corner." She indicated Ivy and Walnut with a nod of her pointed chin. "I already took care of it. Talked to the principal of Belltown Intermediate myself."

"But, Mom, someone already lives here. The school's going to find out—"

"The Costas, José, and Roberta. They stay here summers and winter in Miami. They have two grown sons, but the boys don't come home to visit much. Nobody ever sees the Costas, and of course they don't belong to the country club. Latinos." She looked at her daughter, obviously pleased with herself. "I did my research. I was careful to pick the right house."

"But what about my friends?"

"You'll have to break from your old friends. They were the wrong kind anyway. Your new friends will think you live here. They can't come over, but that's all right, because you need to go to their houses. Swim in their pools. Play tennis on their courts. Somebody brings you home from choir after school, this is where they drop you off. You disobey me, and there'll be no going out until you graduate from high school."

"Then I'm supposed to walk home?" The idea was laughable, but she could tell by the determined look on her mother's face that she was utterly serious. "Mom." Maggie stared at her. "That's lying."

"Yeah, well, maybe it is, but this is the only way I know to get you ahead. People see the dump we live in, even the new dump, they won't take you seriously, Maggie. Rich people like rich friends. It's the only way you'll ever be one of them. The only way you'll get invited to their parties. The only way you'll get into a decent college. The only way you'll get to medical school."

Maggie came to a halt on the sidewalk in front of 107 Ivy Drive, the same brick Colonial her mother had brought her to the summer she was eleven. Slinging her purse over her other shoulder, she stared at the house beyond the picket fence. Nothing had changed, except that now Maggie thought of it as her house in a dreamy kind of way. She enjoyed waiting for the tulips and daffodils to bloom in the spring, worried about whether or not the grass was getting enough water, and in the winter, she prayed no pipes would break while the real owners were in Florida.

Maggie knew the whole charade was dishonest, but as the years passed, she had come to realize that this house on Ivy Drive insulated her from her family and the world she had built beyond them.

Maggie heard a horn beep as a red convertible rounded the corner, music blasting. The driver waved.

Maggie waved back. Praying she wasn't still perspiring, she walked to the edge of the curb just as Jarrett pulled up.

"Jump in." Jarrett revved the engine as Maggie climbed into the seat beside her and pulled the door shut. "Centerfold" was blaring on the radio.

To cover her nervousness, Maggie made an event of searching for her seat belt and fastening it, singing along with the J. Geils Band. Jarrett was so good looking, with his short blond hair and suntanned face, that he reminded her of one of the Greek gods she'd read about in her classical civilizations class. With his high cheekbones, aquiline nose, and even, white teeth, he had the best smile she'd thought she'd ever see. And at this moment, his smile was directed at her.

"What? You don't want me to meet your folks or anything?" He waited until her buckle clicked before he pulled away from the curb at a reasonable speed. "I don't mind."

Maggie dropped her purse onto the floor, scanning the dash, afraid if she looked at Jarrett she'd say or do something really stupid. He was *so* nice. "Nah. Mom's volunteering at the hospital, then bridge club." She was amazed at how smoothly the line came to her lips. Bridge? Ruth Turner couldn't have played a hand of bridge to save herself from falling off one. "Dad's . . . busy."

She ran her hand over the tan dash that had obviously just been wiped down with some type of upholstery cleaner. She couldn't help wondering if he'd done it for her benefit. She hoped so.

Maggie dared a quick look in his direction. He was dressed in a pair of beach shorts and a light blue polo shirt that matched his heavenly blue eyes. A pair of expensive sunglasses rested on the bridge of his nose.

"You like the car?"

"Love it."

As they rode through the streets of Belltown, laughing and somehow finding things to talk about, Maggie's nervousness began to ease. She liked Jarrett because he wasn't just another good-looking guy from the rich side of Belltown. He had character. He had a good sense of humor. He had morals. And Jarrett didn't just talk about himself. He asked her questions about herself and was genuinely interested in her answers. When Maggie admitted hesitantly that her dream was to become a physician, Jarrett never blinked. He never laughed it her. All he did was smile that handsome smile of his and say she'd make a good doctor.

That night as Jarrett said good-bye to her on the sidewalk beneath the streetlight at 107 Ivy Drive, he kissed her, and Maggie melted in his arms. She was in love. By the time she waved good-bye and watched him drive off in his convertible, she already had another date with Jarrett McKay.

TWO

The summer passed with unbelievable speed for Maggie. Before she knew it, it was late August and she'd soon be returning to Belltown High for her senior year and Jarrett would be going back to college. Just the thought of not seeing Jarrett every day made her heart ache. She loved him so much.

They hadn't spent a day apart since their first date. They went to movies, swam in his parents' pool, and went to pork roast luaus at the country club. Maggie watched Jarrett compete in tennis matches and he came to the stables to watch her ride. When Jarrett's family went to stay in their beach house, he refused to go without her, and she was invited to go along.

Maggie and Jarrett spent a magical summer getting to know each other and falling in love. He introduced her to his family and though he asked about hers, he didn't press her. Jarrett met Ruth only once, and that was at a horse show. She had made a fuss over him, embarrassing Maggie to death. After that, Maggie made sure she kept Jarrett away from her family. She used the excuse that her parents didn't really approve of her dating Jarrett exclusively. It was only a half lie. The truth was Ruth had been badgering her daughter to date other guys she'd met through Jarrett. Her mother hadn't wanted Maggie and Jarrett to become serious.

Maggie pulled her beach bag from the closet she shared with her sister and began to pack, trying to think over the sound of her sister's rock music.

"Where's your rich boyfriend taking you now?" Lisa asked from the bed where she lay sprawled, painting her toenails with fluorescent pink nail polish.

Maggie glanced over her shoulder at her sister. Lisa's bleached-beyond-repair hair was piled on her head in hot rollers. Her eyes were so heavily made up with black eyeliner that she reminded Maggie of a raccoon. She was dressed in a halter top, her breasts more visible than not. Dark pubic hair peeked from the crotch of her short shorts.

"I said, where you goin', Mags?" She nodded her head to the pounding beat of the heavy metal rockers.

"To the beach." Maggie picked up her one-piece bathing suit and dropped it into her bag. She didn't want to get into an argument with Lisa.

"Ah, the beach. Mr. Rich Boy's beach house on the shore, of course." Her nails done, Lisa reached under the double bed the two girls shared and drew out an ashtray.

"Please don't smoke in here," Maggie said. She hated the stench of the smoke from her mother's cigarettes, and her room was the one place she could escape it.

Lisa lit up with exaggerated pleasure and leaned back against the scratched headboard to take a drag.

Maggie hurriedly stuffed a hairbrush and her makeup kit into her beach bag. The more she said to Lisa, the worse her sister was. She just had to ignore her. "Have you seen my sweatshirt, Lisa? The one Jarrett gave me."

"Don't know what you're talking about." She blew a perfect smoke ring from her pursed red lips. "Never seen it."

"Oh, you have so. It's gray and says Georgetown U. on it." She dropped a hand on her hip, turning to face her sister. She waved at the smoke in the air. "Please, Lisa. I left it right on the dresser. It's cold on the beach. I might need it."

"So why not get that rich boy to keep you warm?" Lisa lifted plucked and penciled eyebrow suggestively.

Maggie frowned. She didn't know what the problem between her and her sister was. They had never gotten along particularly well, even as children, but it was getting worse. Ever since Maggie began dating Jarrett, Lisa had been more confrontational than usual. "Forget it. I'll borrow one of Jarrett's. I've got to go."

"I'll borrow one of Jarrett's," Lisa mimicked as she jumped off the bed to follow Maggie out of their bedroom. She didn't even bother to put out her cigarette.

Maggie waved at the smoke as she went down the hallway. "Criminy, Lisa. You look like Mom." She stopped at the living room archway and stuck her head around the corner. Ruth was sitting on the couch in her housecoat, watching her soap opera, her feet propped on a pile of newspapers. "Going, Mother. We're going to his beach house in Delaware."

Ruth waved, then looked back in Maggie's direction. "Are you smoking again in my house, Lisa Turner?"

Maggie looked back into the hallway, where her sister stood puffing on her cigarette.

"No, Mother. I wouldn't do that."

"Good," Ruth called. Then she turned back to the TV and both daughters were dismissed.

Maggie secretly vowed to herself when she was a mother, she'd do a better job. Oh, yes, Ruth was concerned about Maggie if she missed a tennis lesson or didn't get on the cheerleading squad, but there was no emotional attachment. Some days Maggie wondered if her mother loved her at all.

Lisa might as well have not existed. Ever since junior high, she had hung out with "the wrong crowd." She drank. She smoked. Through her high school years, she came and went as she pleased. When she dropped out the middle of her senior year, Ruth barely blinked. "I expected as much," she'd commented as she'd hung wet clothes on the line to dry.

Maggie went down the hallway toward the kitchen, her beach bag flung over her shoulder.

"What, you're not even going to say good-bye to your sister?" Lisa taunted.

" 'Bye, sister." Maggie went out the back door. The screen door slammed behind her.

"Say," Lisa called after her, pushing open the door again. Her tone had softened. "Me and Rick are goin' up to the pits tonight. Us and some friends. We got beer. I might even give you underagers a sip or two. Want to come?"

"Can't. Jarrett and I are meeting his friends at the

beach. His parents got a permit for a bonfire." Maggie cut across the lawn that needed mowing. "Hope you have a good time."

Lisa let the screen door slam shut. "Yeah, right," she uttered.

Maggie sat close to Jarrett on the beach blanket, enjoying the weight of his arm wrapped casually around her shoulder. A bonfire illuminated the quiet beach with jagged yellow light. Red cinders rose like fireflies into the air, cracking and popping. The half moon hung low in the sky, blazing a path across the water. In the distance she could hear the steady ebb and flow of the tide as the ocean rushed onto the beach.

One of Jarrett's college friends played his guitar and some others sang a slow and mournful Billy Joel song.

Jarrett lifted a beer to his lips, took a sip, and then leaned over to kiss her on the cheek, while talking to the friend sitting next to him.

Maggie smiled and wished the night could go on forever. She loved the beach. She loved the salty smell that hung in the air and the rhythm of the waves. Someday this was where she was going to live. When she was a physician, she'd be able to afford a house like the McKays'. Maybe even live in it with Jarrett.

The song ended and Jarrett's best friend Zach set aside his guitar. "How 'bout another brewsky?" He opened the ice chest sunk in the sand and pulled out a bottle of cold beer.

"I'll take one," his girlfriend said. "Me, too," someone else called from the shadows.

Zach stood to pass out the beer, swaying on his feet. "Maggie?"

"No, thanks." She smiled and lifted her diet soda. "I'm fine." She didn't like beer. It reminded her too much of her father, asleep in a stupor in his chair, or Lisa, who got drunk five out of seven nights a week.

"Maggie's drinking soda?" He turned to Jarrett. "Say, what's with your girl, Jarrett? I know you said she was just a kid, but come on."

She felt Jarrett tense beside her. His hand rubbed her shoulder. "She said no thanks."

"Come on. It's a party. The girl's gotta have a beer." He stepped in front of them and leaned over to Jarrett in feigned confidentiality. "How else you gonna get a little pussy, eh, old buddy?"

Jarrett jumped up, knocking his own beer over. Before Maggie could stop him, he drew back his fist and slammed Zach in the jaw.

Zach fell backward into the sand, the beer meant for Maggie flying out of his hand and landing in the bonfire. "Why did you do that?" Zach stumbled to his feet, nursing his jaw.

"Because, *asshole,* you don't talk like that around girls, and because, *asshole,* she said she doesn't want a beer."

Maggie jumped to her feet, not knowing what to do. Zach was Jarrett's best friend; they were fraternity brothers. She put her hand on Jarrett's bare back. "It's OK, Jarrett," she said softly. "He's drunk. You didn't have to hit him for my sake."

Jarrett drew back his fist again. "Sure I did. Maybe he needs another, eh, Zach?"

Zach stumbled to the ice chest and pulled out another beer. "Man, what's gotten into you, Jarrett, old buddy?" He gave a loud, exaggerated belch. "I just wanted everyone to have a little fun. Can't have fun without beer."

Jarrett grabbed Maggie's hand. "Let's go for a walk. I've had enough of these jerks."

Maggie grabbed her towel off the sand and trudged behind Jarrett, letting him lead her by the hand. "Sorry about that," Jarrett said, kicking sand. "Zach's not a bad a guy. Just drinks too much."

"It's all right. I could have handled him myself." She glanced at Jarrett sideways, smiling shyly. "But thanks for coming to my rescue anyway."

Jarrett stopped and turned to face her. It was so natural for Maggie to let him wrap her in his arms. She lifted her chin to meet his kiss.

"God, I'm going to miss you when I have to go back to school," he murmured against her lips.

He tasted like beer and himself, a man's taste. "I'll miss you, too," she whispered.

"I'll come home every weekend I can." This time he kissed the tip of her nose.

Maggie wrapped her arms around Jarrett's waist, letting the towel she'd thrown over her shoulders float to the ground. Her blood raced as she pressed her breasts against his bare chest. Even through the damp material of her swimsuit, she could feel her nipples growing hard. These were all new experiences for her. No one had ever touched her the way she let Jarrett touch her. It had never felt right before.

Maggie pressed her lips to his, teasing him with the tip of her tongue. He slid his hand into the top of her suit and she sighed as his thumb brushed her puckered nipple. She parted her lips, welcoming his tongue into her mouth, all hot and wet. His other hand wound her hair around his fingers.

"Maggie, I love you," Jarrett whispered when their mouths separated.

"I love you, too," she whispered.

Jarrett slipped his hand out of her suit and leaned over to pick up the towel she'd dropped. "Let's sit over here out of the light and talk."

Maggie laughed, running to catch up with him. "Talk," she teased, "or grope?"

He laughed with her, his rich, masculine voice sending shivers of pleasure through her. "OK. A little groping, a little talking."

Still laughing, she plopped down beside him on the towel he'd spread in the sand, just out of reach of the incoming tide. They sat hand in hand with the dunes to their backs, the ocean washing onto the shore directly in front of them. Jarrett picked up a bucket and shovel left behind by some child, and began to fill the bucket with sand. "What are we going to do about dating when we go back to school, Maggie?" He dumped the sand from the bucket onto the beach in a smooth tower.

She watched him create another tower in the sand.

She had known this discussion was coming. She'd rehearsed what she was going to say over and over again, but now she couldn't remember her lines.

Even if he said he loved her, she couldn't ask Jarrett not to date other girls at college. It wouldn't be mature of her. Still, what did she want to be, mature or nuts? Just the thought of Jarrett kissing someone else made her crazy.

"What do *you* want to do?" she hedged.

He went on building his sandcastle, creating a wall with his capable hands. "You haven't dated that much, Maggie. I'm sure there are guys at Belltown High you'd—"

"Are we talking about me or you?" she asked pointedly. "Because I already know there's no one in Belltown I want to swap spit with. Too many germs."

He tipped back his head and laughed as he formed a moat around his castle with the red plastic shovel. "You're going to make a great doctor, Maggie. You've got that unromantic, clinical way about you."

She rested her head on his shoulder. "Seriously," she said, brushing his cheek with her fingertips, "you're older than I am; I'm still in high school. I'm sure there are some great college girls—"

He dropped the toy shovel and bucket and brushed the sand from his hands. "I didn't meet anyone like you at Georgetown, Maggie."

She smiled. Looking into his blue eyes made her heart sing. "Good. I hope it stays that way, but we probably should leave it open." She lifted her shoulder. "If you meet someone you want to go out with, then go out with her."

"And if you meet someone"—he poked her between her breasts with his finger—"you'll go out with him."

"Yeah, right." She laid on her back to look up at the stars. "Like I'd want to date Mark Little or Derek Smelton. Their feet are too big and their voices are still changing."

He chuckled and stretched out on the towel beside her. "Look what I made for you." He pointed at the sand castle.

"Oh, it's beautiful," she breathed. Then she looked at him, suddenly somber. "But it won't stand long. The tide's coming in. The water's going to wash it away."

"So I'll build you another one. As many as you like. For the rest of my life, every time we come to the beach, I'll build you a sandcastle. Even when we're old and we have to hobble onto the beach with our walkers."

"Don't make promises like that," she whispered. "We shouldn't make promises we might not be able to keep."

He kissed her temple. "Maggie, Maggie, you're so serious sometimes. What am I going to do with you?"

She looked at him. She didn't know why the sandcastle bothered her so much. It just did. She didn't want the ocean to take it away. "You could kiss me," she whispered.

Without answering, he lowered his mouth over hers. When he came up for breath, she brushed back a lock of his damp hair. "Thanks for the castle and thanks again for being my hero, Jarrett."

He leaned over to kiss her, pressing her into the still warm sand. His voice was a whisper of genuine emotion. "I hope I always will be."

THREE

The Present

Maggie sat down in the sand, drew her knees up, and wrapped the light blanket around her as much for comfort as to ward off the morning chill. The sun was just rising in all its glory over the lip of the endless ocean, all bright and yellow, a burning ball of gasses and light—the most magical time of day at the beach.

Only Maggie couldn't feel the magic. She couldn't feel anything but the numbness that had invaded her three days before, when she'd received news of Stanley's and Jordan's deaths.

"I brought tea and muffins." Kyle approached from behind her, a picnic basket swinging over one arm. On the other, like a maître d', he carried a small checkered tablecloth. In his usual neat, fashionable style, he wore pristine white jeans rolled above his ankles and a red polo. A white tennis sweater was draped over his shoulders. "How about some tea, Maggie dear?"

"No. No tea. Nothing for me."

"Horse-hocky." Kyle spread out the red-and-white gingham tablecloth, its corners fluttering in the salty breeze before they came to rest in the sand. "You've got to eat to keep up your strength."

Maggie said nothing as Kyle sat beside her in the sand and spread out the morning fare. He had a plate of homemade cinnamon apple muffins just out of the oven and a tub of butter. From a thermos, he poured a mug of tea for each of them. "Earl Grey with lemon, no sugar, no milk. Just as you like it."

When Maggie made no attempt to take the steaming mug, Kyle gently pressed it into her hand. "Drink, Maggie."

Because it was easier than arguing with Kyle, Maggie took a sip from the blue, salt-glazed mug. The tea, though tasteless to her palate, warmed her from the inside. Still, it couldn't chase the chill from her heart. She stared at the waves breaking on the shore. It would be low tide soon. Teens would be out on their skim boards, taking advantage of the pools of water that lay on the beach only at low tide and the fact that the lifeguards weren't on duty yet.

Kyle sat beside her and sipped his tea. "Penny for your thoughts."

Maggie watched a wave crest and break, pouring like water from a cup. She couldn't stop thinking of Stanley and Jordan. "This is all my fault."

"Of course it is, dear." Kyle set his tea down carefully on the tablecloth and reached for a plate and a muffin. "You were driving that Jeep like a bat out of hell on the beltway. You saw the red Mazda, but you'd had one too many vodka and tonics at happy hour. You just couldn't brake in time."

Maggie shook her head, staring but not really seeing. "I never should have married Stanley."

"You're right. Too dour. Too controlled. I told you that years ago. I make it habit never to date men named Stanley."

Maggie swallowed another sip of tea. "I never really loved him, Kyle." *Not the way I loved Jarrett,* she thought, and then wondered where the hell that came from. "He was convenient. Comfortable. But I didn't love him."

"Sure you did. Eat." He put a plate in front of her. The blue plate contrasted well with the tablecloth. It was Kyle's way. The muffin was already cut and glistening with butter.

"I didn't love him." She exhaled so that her un-combed bangs fluttered. "Well, I mean I loved him like I love my old barn coat. Like I love my slipper socks with the hole in the toe. But I didn't love him with a passion—not like a person loves a red convertible."

Kyle took a bite of his muffin and reached for a cloth napkin to wipe the corner of his mouth. "Excuse me if I'm slow-witted at six in the morning, but are you comparing your deceased husband to a sports car?"

Maggie couldn't resist a sad smile. What would she have done without Kyle these last three days? Gone mad, probably. "You know . . . the way the wind blows your hair when you ride with the top down. The way you can feel the speed. The way it makes your heart pound every time you start the engine."

"I once dated a guy who made me feel like that."

Maggie glanced over at her dearest friend. "And what happened to him?"

It was Kyle's turn to stare off into the distance. "He dumped me for a cheeky blond lobbyist." He chased a crumb across the salt-glazed plate with his finger. "Never met another like him. Still looking, though."

Maggie's gaze met Kyle's. Dampness glistened in his eyes, making her tear up. She looked away.

"Hell." He took her hand. "I'm supposed to be here comforting you, and instead I'm talking about my lousy love life."

"It's certainly more interesting than my own." To pacify Kyle, she picked up half her muffin and took a nibble. Despite the heavenly aroma, it tasted like sawdust in her mouth. She chewed and swallowed out of reflex. "I feel so damned guilty, Kyle. I made him unhappy."

"You didn't. Stanley was as happy as Stanley could ever have been."

"He didn't want children."

"He loved Jordan. Don't let your grief-stricken head tell you otherwise. He loved his son, your son."

"Yes. He came to love him." Maggie's chest felt so heavy that it ached. "But Jordan was an inconvenience. Stanley was meant to be a bachelor. He didn't adjust well to puke on his Armani coat and three a.m. feedings. I convinced him we should marry and have children because *my* biological clock was ticking."

"I was there. You didn't arm wrestle him down the aisle. And as far as Jordan's conception, it takes two to rhumba, love."

Maggie ran her hand over her face. "When I told him I wanted another baby when Jordan was only a few months old, you should have seen the look on his face. He suggested getting a puppy. When the results of my testing came back and Dr. Naylor said there wasn't a chance in hell I would ever get pregnant again, Stanley couldn't hide the relief in his voice. Instead of giving me a baby, he took me to Paris. I cried the whole week we were there. I ruined his trip."

"Stanley *wasn't* unhappy." Kyle finished off his muffin and wiped his mouth with his napkin. "You were, maybe, but not Stanley. I don't mean to speak ill of the dead, but if you ask me, he didn't have enough emotional substance to *be* unhappy. The man was a robot."

Maggie reached for her mug of tea again. It was actually beginning to taste good. "I know you never liked him, but he was good for me. He came into my life at a point when I needed his stability."

"He came at a time when you needed some sperm from a decent gene pool."

Maggie frowned.

"I mean, he just never seemed right for you, " Kyle continued. "When you talked about Stanley, you never got the shine in your eyes you had the night you got drunk and told me about the boy you dated in high school."

Maggie groaned and lowered her head to her bent knees. That was twice in one day she'd been reminded of Jarrett—a raw wound that had been pacified by antacids and denial, but had never healed. "I did not *get drunk.*"

"Say, wasn't this where you used to come with him? Where you fell in love?" Kyle rattled on as he cleaned up the breakfast stuff, leaving her plate in the hope, she knew, that she might eat another bite or two. "It was this beach, wasn't it? You said his folks had a place."

Maggie knew what Kyle was trying to do. He was trying to get her to think about something other than the funeral today, something other than her baby boy cremated, his ashes in a jar. What he didn't know was that the subject of Jarrett was almost as deep a wound, just not as fresh.

"Just a few blocks from here," she said softly.

"Your first puppy love. I remember mine. Jason Rickers. He was in my drama class my sophomore year of high school."

Puppy love. Maggie's chest tightened. Kyle went on telling her about his Jason, but she wasn't really listening. For a moment she allowed herself to think of Jarrett. She remembered that night at the beach just before he'd gone back to college when, so young and in love, with their whole lives ahead of them, they'd rolled in the sand. Touching. Kissing. Discovering.

After all these years, she could still vividly remember the shivers of pleasure she had felt when Jarrett's mouth had touched her breast. She remembered wanting to make love to him that night. She remembered Jarrett was the one who said they should wait and be sure it was right. Jarrett, always the hero.

She had never let Stanley be her hero. Another reason to feel guilty.

"Of course, he never knew I had a crush on him," Kyle finished with a sigh of loves lost. "He wasn't gay, so I never had a chance with him. But heavens, how I enjoyed playing that scene from *Death Of A Salesman* with him."

Maggie glanced at Kyle. He was model handsome, well groomed, and not the least bit effeminate in appearance. "I think I'll go up to the house now," she said. Her voice was ghostly in her ears. Unreal. This was *all* unreal. "Get a shower. Get ready."

"Maggie, it's only six. You have plenty of time before we need to head to DC. The memorial service isn't for nine hours."

"I know, but I need to go by the hospital. There was a patient I admitted—"

"The hospital can function without you." He stood, brushing the sand off his jeans, then offered her a hand.

Maggie rose, bringing her blanket with her to shield herself from the first vacationers appearing on the beach. Beneath the blanket she was dressed in nothing but panties and an old T-shirt of Stanley's. There seemed to be no reason to dress.

Maggie started up the dunes, following the path that led off the beach and onto the street where her oceanfront house stood.

Kyle scooped up the remainder of the breakfast and ran to catch up with her. "I really think you should let me drive you to DC. This is silly. You're going. I'm going. If nothing else, it's a waste of fossil fuel."

She looked at him. She felt so tired. So old. *No thirty-three year old should have to feel this way.* "I just want to be alone, Kyle. I don't want you to see me a wreck. Crying."

He looped her arm through his and escorted her up

the sandy path. "That's half your trouble. You haven't cried enough."

She pushed back a lock of her shoulder-length hair. It was dirty and tangled. "Kyle, I'm afraid if I start crying, I won't be able to stop. Ever." A sob rose in her throat and she caught it before she made a sound.

Kyle hugged her. "Ah, sweetheart. If I could take the pain from you, I would."

Maggie knew it was true. Kyle was that kind of friend. "I'm a physician," she reasoned aloud. They reached the paved road and turned toward her house. "I deal with death and dying every day. I should be handling this better."

"You're handling it fine."

At her doorway, Maggie stopped and turned to Kyle. "How about if I just meet you in DC at the memorial service? We'll go from there to Stanley's folks' house afterward."

He squeezed her arm. "You sure, hon?"

"I'm sure."

"Three o'clock, right?"

"Yeah. Would you mind calling my mom and dad and reminding them?"

"Not at all."

"You'd better call Lisa, too. Early, before she has her first Bloody Mary. Otherwise she won't make it."

"Don't tell me your entire family will be here."

A faint smile played on her lips. "In all their horror."

Kyle turned away, raising his hand to his forehead in an exaggerated manner. "Let me get my Valium out now. I can tell it's going to be one of *those* days."

Maggie started up the steps to the first floor of her

beach house. "Better bring some along for me, too. I may need it by the end of the day."

He turned back. "You serious? It wouldn't be a bad idea."

She grimaced. "I told you. I told the crisis counselor at the hospital. No drugs. Hell, I'm neurotic enough as it is around my family. I don't need any help." She gave a vague wave and started up the steps again.

"Call me if you need me, or if you change your mind about wanting to ride over with me."

She raised her hand so that Kyle knew she'd heard him and then disappeared into the house. She was going to need all the time she could get to pull herself together before the funeral.

Maggie stood near the coat closet of her in-laws' Alexandria town house, unsteady on her black pumps. Though not a drinking woman, she wished to God she had a vodka and tonic right now. Anything to numb the pain. Anything to get her through the rest of the afternoon.

The memorial service had gone well. Maggie nearly choked on her own thoughts. *As well as any funeral for your husband and child can go.* It had taken place in Stanley's parents' church, the same church Maggie and Stanley had been married in five years earlier.

Because she'd had Stanley's and little Jordan's bodies cremated, there had been no viewing. No small white coffin at the altar. No lilies permeating the air with their death scent. That was how Maggie had wanted it.

There had been an argument from Stanley's parents, but she'd stood her ground. In the end, she'd won.

A children's choir had sung at the funeral, angelic voices floating upward, carrying the souls of her loved ones to heaven, perhaps. Then men and women in dark gray pinstriped suits had walked to the pulpit to proclaim what a fine businessman Stanley had been. They used words like dependable, trustworthy, admirable. No one said Stanley was fun.

When Jordan's day-care mother stood at the pulpit, Maggie had concentrated on the stained glass windows of the opulent church. She had tried to decipher the pictures, excavating past memories of Sunday School, trying to remember the Old Testament stories. Wasn't that Joseph's many-colored coat? And there, near the vestibule, Moses parting the Red Sea? Anything not to hear Miss Jean's voice. Anything not to hear what a sweet, bright, loving child Jordan had been.

Had been. Past tense. Dead. Gone. Ashes to ashes, dust to dust. Maggie didn't cry. She hurt too much to cry.

After the service, Kyle had grabbed her arm and made a beeline for the sanctuary exit. When Stanley's mother caught up to them and suggested Maggie should stand in the receiving line in the narthex, Maggie could have sworn Kyle had used the F word in his hissing response. Something about receiving lines being for f-ing weddings, not a baby's funeral.

Maggie thanked sweet God for Kyle. If she'd had to stand there and shake people's hands, she'd have crumbled.

"Oh, there you are, Maggie, dear." Stanley's parents,

Eunice and Edward, approached her, joined at the hip as they usually were, with only the female of the Siamese twins apparently able to speak. Edward's purpose in life seemed to be to repeat what his wife said. Maggie had always thought they were a strange couple, but then, whose parents who'd been together thirty-five years weren't?

Eunice was clothed in black linen, a new Chanel sheathe for the occasion. Huge diamonds sparkled in her ears. She looked as if she'd recently touched up the makeup around her eyes. So she did have a heart.

"You left the church before us and arrived here late," Eunice chastised. "We were worried about you. You should have ridden with us. Edward had the Cadillac washed and waxed."

"Washed and waxed," Edward echoed.

Maggie pushed back her bangs. She had never liked Stanley's parents when he was living. Did she have to put up with their inane crap now that he was dead? "I stopped at the Kwik-Mart for ibuprofen."

"We have aspirin, dear. I'm hurt you wouldn't want our aspirin."

"Our aspirin," echoed Edward the canyon.

Maggie looked down, the sparkle of her two-carat engagement diamond twinkling up at her. It was an antique from the 1920s; the ring she'd always wanted. She now wondered if the last wearer had been affected so tragically. Maybe that was why the ring had ended up at the art auction where she and Stanley found it. "I just needed a few minutes alone, Eunice." Maggie breathed deeply. "To settle my nerves."

"Well, come in and say hello to everyone. Eat some

ham." Eunice caught her arm and led her across the imported Turkish carpet, down the hall toward the dining room.

"I hate ham," Maggie whispered. "Funeral food."

"Oh, God, Maggie."

Maggie spotted her sister coming out of the dining room. She appeared even thinner than usual, dressed in an expensive black cap-sleeved dress and matching linen heels. Her eyes were red from crying, her dark makeup smudged.

Lisa put out her hand and Maggie took it. Eunice and Edward stopped.

"We'll be in in a minute," Maggie told them cordially.

Her in-law twins moved on.

Lisa squeezed Maggie's hand, her eyes welling up as their gazes met. "I'm so sorry," she managed to sob.

"You said that," Maggie whispered, tired. She didn't know what to say to people or how to accept their condolences gracefully. Being the physician of the family, the one who dealt with death the most, she kept feeling it was her job to console them.

Lisa let go of Maggie's hand and reached into her Paloma Picasso purse. She drew out a leather cigarette case.

Maggie folded her arms over her chest and leaned against the hand-painted wallpaper of the wide hallway. She never quite knew how to deal with her sister, even now that they had become adults. They still didn't see eye to eye. They were just too different.

Lisa was what Kyle called a husbandizer. She was on her fourth marriage, and each man was wealthier than the last. She spent her days going to beauty salons, tanning beds, and psychics. Still, Maggie had to give Lisa credit for being here when she'd needed her. It was Lisa who lived here in DC, Lisa who had met her and the state trooper at the hospital the night Stanley and Jordan died. Lisa had been on the beltway coming home from somewhere. She'd come upon the accident, identified the bodies, and had Maggie contacted.

Maggie rubbed her temples with her thumb and forefinger. "Eunice will have a cow if you smoke in here, Lisa. It'll discolor the Chinese paper." She indicated the wall covered with flowers and leaves with a nod of her chin.

"Screw Eunice." Lisa sniffed back her tears and lit up. She inhaled deeply before she spoke again. "I tried calling you all day yesterday, but all I got was your butler."

"Kyle was handling the phone for me. I just couldn't deal with it."

"He could have let *me* through. I'm your sister, for Christ's sake." She sniffed again and reached into her purse to pull out an embroidered hanky.

"He was only trying to help." Maggie glanced down the hallway toward the dining room. "Where are Mom and Dad?"

"Mom's at the buffet table looking for the largest butterfly shrimp for her plate." She blew smoke. "Dad's in the john with his irritated bowel." She fluttered her heavily mascaraed eyelashes. "Typical."

Her sister had certainly changed a great deal since her high school days and the wild years that followed, but Maggie still saw flashes of the old Lisa. She liked her mascara. She liked her cigarettes. She liked her booze.

"And Martin? Where's your husband?"

"Gone to Geneva. Business. The prick. He said to send his sympathies, but he couldn't possibly get home before the end of the week." She inhaled deeply, making no attempt to hide her bitterness. "Thank Christ I wasn't killed. They'd have had to put me on ice until the Geneva matter was settled." She looked quickly at Maggie, brushing her frail hand against her sister's arm. "Oh, God, I'm sorry, Mags. That was insensitive." She dabbed at her bloodshot eyes. "I just don't know what I'm saying. This hit me hard."

"Tell me about it." Maggie pressed her back to the wall so that two older couples could pass down the hallway. She smiled cordially, though she didn't recognize them.

Lisa touched Maggie's sleeve again. It felt good to Maggie to see her sister really did care about her.

"So how are you?" Lisa asked.

"OK."

"No. I mean *how are you?* I can't imagine how horrible this must be for you. I mean, a husband—he's expendable."

Maggie flashed her a warning glance.

"Well, maybe not a man like Stanley. But a baby, Maggie. Your son." Lisa leaned the back of her head against the wall, careful not to muss her slick, short blond hair. It was still bleached, but at least it was professionally done these days. "I know how you wanted more children. First came the doctor's report, now this. Considering the past—"

Maggie lifted her hand, cutting her off in midsentence. "Lisa, please. I'm hanging together with just a little spit and paste. I can't talk about this. Let's just go into the dining room. I'll get you a drink. Something to eat." She looked at her sister, the same height she was, but twenty pounds lighter. "You could use some protein."

"I'll take the drink, a double," Lisa said. "Screw the shrimp and the horse they came in on."

The two sisters made their way to the dining room, where a catered buffet was spread across three mahogany tables. Maggie mixed her sister a gin and tonic and the two drifted apart in the crowd of nearly fifty people. Maggie made her obligatory greetings. She even nibbled on a cracker. But when she saw her mother coming toward her, she wished she could dig a hole in Eunice's white carpet and hide. She didn't think she was up to dealing Ruth this afternoon.

"Maggie."

"Mother."

Ruth was dressed agreeably in a navy-and-white department store dress. She'd had her hair and nails done. She looked so nice she almost appeared to belong in this dining room. Almost. "Did you eat?"

"Not hungry." Maggie hung onto her diet soda for dear life.

"You should eat. The Brittinghams must have spent a fortune on this layout," she whispered under her breath. She tapped the plate in her hand piled with shrimp. "Royal Doulton."

Maggie rolled her eyes. "Mother. It's a funeral. My

husband and son are dead. Could you refrain from making comments on the china?"

Ruth let out an exasperated sigh. "I was just trying to make conversation. To take your mind off it."

Not once had Ruth told Maggie she was sorry. Not once had she hugged her. She had, however, remembered to ask if Stanley had left her well off financially.

"Oh, there you are, Maggie! I've been looking for you."

Maggie glanced up to see Kyle coming toward her. "I have to speak to you." He smiled graciously at Ruth. "Would you excuse us, Mother Turner?" He didn't wait for an answer, but swept Maggie smoothly away. He didn't stop until they reached the kitchen, which was filled with aproned caterers.

Maggie leaned against a counter, her sigh of relief lifting her bangs. She set down her glass. "Thank you."

"You owe me."

She raised her palm to swear an oath. "I owe you. I'll cut you a break next racquetball match."

"Cut me a break, hah!" He snatched an hors d'oeuvre as a waiter went by with a full tray. "So have we been here long enough?"

Maggie looked up at Kyle. He was dressed sharply as always, as if he'd just stepped off the cover of *GQ*. "I've had enough. I just want to go home and go to bed. I want to pull the sheet over my head and sleep for a week."

Kyle looped her arm through his and led her toward the back door. "You got it."

"Hey, where are we going?"

He opened the door that led outside. "Home."

She glanced over her shoulder. "But don't I need to say good-bye? My parents . . . Eunice and Edward . . ."

"Maggie, darling, you're the grieving widow. You can do what the hell you please." He stopped on the stone steps. "So do you want to go home now or not? Have you had enough?"

She didn't have to think about it. "Yes."

"Then let's go. We'll drive together. It'll be fun. We can call each other on our cellulars and exchange recipes at forty-two cents a minute."

Maggie had to chuckle as she slipped past Kyle into the driver's seat of her green Jag. But somehow the laughter seemed a betrayal to her son's name. A weight pressed on her shoulders, spreading to her heart and her lungs, preventing her from breathing deeply. As she slipped on her sunglasses and shoved the key into the ignition, she couldn't help wondering if she would ever laugh again without this heaviness.

FOUR

December, 1983

"Jingle bells, jingle bells, jingle all the way," Maggie sang as she sat cross-legged on her lumpy bed wrapping Jarrett's Christmas present. "Oh, what fun it is to ride in a one-horse open sleigh."

"Oh, please, spare me the holiday joy. There are homeless people sleeping in alleys tonight while you sing about riding through the snow in your friggin' little red sleigh." Lisa walked into their bedroom, a cigarette hanging from her ruby lips.

Ruth had given up trying to prevent her from smoking in the house months ago. Despite Maggie's protests against smoking in the bedroom they shared, Ruth had said if Lisa was old enough to pay taxes and fight in a war, she could smoke a harmless cigarette. Neither Maggie's reminder that women couldn't get drafted nor her review of the dangers of secondhand smoke would budge her mother.

Maggie stopped singing, but went on wrapping. She refused to let Lisa and her cynicism spoil her evening. Tonight was Maggie's first night with Jarrett in two weeks, and she couldn't wait to see him. Over the phone, he'd told her he'd planned a special night, but he wouldn't say where they were going. All he said was to put on her best dress and dancing heels and he'd pick her up at six. Maggie would have to hustle if she was going to dress, curl her hair, and make it to Ivy Drive by then.

Lisa slipped into a short black leather skirt and red-glitter tube top. She had piled her hair on top of her head, dyed in several unnatural shades of red. The *new* Lisa, she said. She had gotten her GED but quit Belltown Community College at Halloween—quit or flunked out. Maggie didn't know which. But now Lisa was enrolled in Miss Sue's School of Hair and Nail Design. She came home every Wednesday with her hair in a different style, and on Fridays the color changed. Maggie guessed no one was brave enough to let Lisa Turner do their hair, so she was forced to experiment on herself.

Lisa came over to the bed and tried to peek under the wrapping paper. "What you got there? Something for me?"

Maggie reached for the tape, sealing the end of the shirt box. "A gift for Jarrett."

Lisa lifted a plucked, penciled eyebrow. "A present for Jarrett? Now what could you buy the little rich boy that his mummy and daddy haven't already bought him?"

"It's a ski sweater," Maggie admitted begrudgingly. "And a picture of us from this fall." She pushed the framed five-by-seven photograph across the bed. It showed Maggie and Jarrett in a wheelbarrow of leaves. She was on his lap and they were laughing.

Lisa barely glanced at the picture and then flopped down in the yellow vinyl beanbag chair. "A picture of the two of you in each other's arms. How sweet. 'Course, the question is will Rich Boy be laughing when he finds out you don't live in that fancy house on Ivy?"

"I don't think that would matter to Jarrett." Maggie reached for the picture and began to wrap it in red and green Santa paper. She already felt guilty enough about deceiving him. She didn't want to talk about it with Lisa.

"Oh, no, it won't matter now, as long as you're a good lay, but I hope you're not expecting anything more out of Richie Rich."

Maggie knew she blushed. She and Lisa never discussed sex, though Lisa often commented on the subject, trying to find out if Maggie was doing it with Jarrett. She'd even offered to make an appointment at the clinic for Maggie to get birth control pills. Of course Maggie knew her sister had been sleeping around for years. Lisa kept condoms in her purse and left them lying around the bedroom, probably to embarrass Maggie.

Maggie jumped up off the bed, her gifts wrapped. She had to get ready. It wasn't Lisa's business if she and Jarrett were having sex or not. The truth was, they weren't. Well, they hadn't gone all the way. But Maggie knew their relationship was going to reach that point soon. She could feel it every time she was in Jarrett's arms. And it wasn't just Jarrett who was getting anxious. She was, too. She loved Jarrett—loved him enough to know she wanted to spend the rest of her life with him. So what if she was young? That was how she felt. That was how Jarrett felt about her.

"Oh, come on. Look at you, all red-faced." Lisa turned in the chair, staring at Maggie. "Don't tell me you still haven't done the dirty deed." She laughed, throwing up her hands, showing off her fire-engine-red press-on nails.

Maggie turned away, pulling her new black dress out of the closet. "That's none of your business."

Lisa cackled. "Oh, Mags, you're such a prude. If your rich boy isn't up to it, I could point you in the direction of some guys—"

Maggie grabbed her new black bra and bikini panties, a pair of hose, and her black heels from the top of her cluttered dresser. She didn't want to hear what her sister had to say. Not only was Lisa embarrassing her, she was making her angry. What she and Jarrett did was out of love, but somehow Lisa made it sound sick, degrading.

"Hey, where are you going?" Lisa dropped her cigarette butt into a soda can.

"The bathroom, where I can dress in peace." Maggie flounced off. Behind her, she could hear Lisa laughing as she slammed the bathroom door.

Jarrett picked Maggie up in front of the house on Ivy Drive at precisely six. It was dark and cold out, with a half moon shining bright. It had just begun to snow, the powdery flakes falling lightly.

"Hey," Jarrett called to her as he leaned across the passenger seat and pushed open the door. "I told you I'd come in to get you. It's too cold out for you to be waiting for me."

Maggie slipped into the seat beside him, his gifts in her arms. She pressed her mouth to his, silencing him. "We've been over this, so shut up, will you? I don't want them near you."

Jarrett groaned as their lips parted. "Maggie, we've been dating seven months. Don't you think I should at least meet your father and sister?"

"They're as bad as my mother. My sister's worse. I don't want them to spoil anything. I've told you that a million times, so let's not talk about it, please?"

"All right, all right. I won't bring it up again. Tonight."

Maggie closed the car door and reached for her seat belt. Only then did she realize Jarrett was wearing a tux. "Pretty fancy," she teased as he pulled away from the curb.

"Like it?" He gave her his best debonair James Bond look. "My mom bought it for me to wear to my cousin Henry's wedding last year."

She rubbed the sleeve of the black jacket. "I love it! So where are we going all spiffed up?"

"It's a surprise." He reached out and draped his arm around her shoulder, hugging her.

Maggie shivered with pleasure at his touch. No matter how often he touched her these days, it was never enough. "I can't wait."

For the next twenty minutes they chatted about his finals coming up, her part in the Christmas play at

Belltown High, what they were going to do during the week between Christmas and New Year's. They laughed and touched, truly happy to be together again. In her excitement, Maggie paid no attention to where they were going until Jarrett pulled into a driveway between two white iron gates. Ahead loomed the McKays' sprawling white house with its massive white columns. It reminded Maggie of Tara in *Gone With the Wind*.

She glanced at him. "You forget something?"

Jarrett grinned as he maneuvered the red car down the snowy driveway. "Nope."

Maggie rubbed at the frosted window so she could see out. The three-story Greek Revival-style house was strangely dark. She looked at Jarrett. "Nobody's home?"

"Nope." He wheeled around the circular drive and stopped in front of the pillared porch. "That's the surprise. Mom and Dad went skiing in Vail." He pulled the emergency brake. "Won't be home until Christmas morning. Three days." He jumped out of the car and ran around to the passenger's side to help her.

Maggie pushed the gifts into his arms and climbed out, a little unsteady in her heels in the slick snow. "You've got the house to yourself for three days? Wow."

"We've got the house all to ourselves." On the top step, Jarrett stopped and pulled Maggie against him with his free hand. Their mouths met and the moment her lips touched his, she realized what this meant. They could be alone together. They could be here alone and undisturbed to do what they wanted, whatever that might be . . .

Suddenly Maggie was giddy with apprehensive excitement. She stepped away from Jarrett and hurried toward the front door. "Come on. I'm cold."

Using his key, he let them in and closed the door behind them, locking it. In the darkness, Maggie heard him drop the gifts on the mahogany table in the entryway and come toward her. She giggled nervously as he reached for her, touching her breast with his fingertips before he caught her.

"Oh, Maggie, I've missed you so much." He kissed her harder this time.

Maggie let him push her against the door as she wrapped her arms around his neck, parting her lips. Their tongues met and Jarrett raised his knee to rub between her thighs. It felt so good. His kiss was hot and wet and filled with desire for her. He made her feel wanted. He made her feel grown-up.

When the kiss ended, Jarrett hung on to Maggie, hugging her. "I really have missed you," he whispered. "I'm not just saying that."

She stroked his back. "I've missed you, too, Jarrett."

"Now, want to see my surprise?" He flipped on the light switch. The room was filled with light from the crystal chandelier.

Maggie squinted in the brightness. "Sure."

He grabbed her hand, leading her through the maze of rooms. With only three people living in the house—Jarrett's older brother had already started med school—Maggie had never understood the McKays' need for a six-bedroom, four-bath house, but a lot of things Jarrett's parents did didn't make sense to her.

When they reached the dining room, Jarrett flipped

on another light. The cherry table with seating for twelve was set at one end for a formal dinner, complete with a white tablecloth. Two white china plates with gold trim had been laid out. There were fluted wine and water glasses and enough gold-plated silverware at each place setting to feed an army.

Maggie walked to the far end of the dining room and picked up one of the white linen napkins. It had been folded into a swan. She turned to Jarrett, holding up the napkin by its delicate white neck. She was touched. Jarrett did love her, *really* loved her. A man didn't make napkins into swans for just anyone. She looked at him. "You did this?"

"Yup." He stuffed his hands into his pockets and suddenly didn't seem so sure of himself, tux or no tux. "It wasn't that hard. My mom has this book. She does that kind of dumb stuff for dinner parties all the time."

Maggie couldn't stop smiling. "The table looks beautiful. You did a great job. Are we having burgers?"

"Nope. Only the best for my Maggie." He crossed the hardwood floor, again the confident Jarrett she knew as he pulled out a chair for her. "You wait right here. I'll be your server this evening, *madame.*"

A moment later he appeared through the swinging kitchen door with two glasses of chilled shrimp cocktail and a bottle of wine.

"Shrimp?" Jarrett knew how much she liked seafood.

"Shrimp for our appetizer, with a fine dry Chardonnay out of Dad's wine cellar."

Her eyes grew round. "You stole wine from your dad?"

"He'll never miss it." He set the fragile glass-stemmed bowl in the center of her dinner plate. "And for our entree, there's filet of sole with broccoli spears and a twice-baked potato." He poured them both a glass of wine and then took the chair at the head of the table.

"I can't believe you did all this." Maggie squeezed his hand as she dipped the first shrimp into cocktail sauce and took a bite.

"Because I love you," he answered, smiling. "Because I wanted our first Christmas together to be memorable."

They shared the splendid dinner Jarrett had orchestrated, laughing and talking. They opened a second bottle of wine. Then, without bothering to clear away the dishes, he swept her into the music room, where he told her that, as a child, he was forced to practice the piano every day. Within minutes, Jarrett had a fire blazing in the granite fireplace and music wafting from hidden speakers in the walls. He took her wineglass from her hand and set it on the mantel.

"May I have this dance?" He held his hand out to her and Maggie accepted it.

"Wait," she whispered. "I'll trip after all the wine." She kicked off her high heels, tossing them into the air so that they hit the polished hardwood floor and slid under the upholstered Chippendale settee.

Jarrett tucked her into his arms and they slow-danced. They kissed. They touched. It was the most magical night Maggie had ever experienced.

"Enjoy your dinner?" Jarrett kissed her temple as he swayed to the music. He was an excellent dancer, but then he excelled at anything he did.

"Wonderful," Maggie breathed. It felt so good to

have his arms around her. She felt so safe and confident. Jarrett made her feel as if she could do anything. Maybe his own self-confidence was wearing off on her.

Their bodies moved to the music, hip against hip, his hands grazing over the tight black dress to caress her back, her buttocks.

When Maggie lifted her chin to kiss Jarrett, there was an urgency in his touch, an urgency that spread to her as their tongues met and twisted.

"I love you, Maggie," he whispered. "I'll love you forever."

"You don't have to say these things. You don't have to make promises—"

"But I want to." He grabbed her shoulders and leaned back to look into her eyes. "I've been thinking a lot about this lately, and I want to make promises. I want to promise I'll always love you. I want to promise that when you're ready, I'll marry you."

Tears welled up in the corners of her eyes. Maggie knew all the arguments. She could hear her mother's voice. *You're both too young. It's puppy love. He's just trying to rebel against his parents.* But none of that changed how Maggie felt in her heart. None of that changed the fact Jarrett felt the same way.

"So will you? Marry me?"

"Oh, Jarrett, I will marry you."

"You think you'll still want me after you become a famous doctor?"

She lifted up on her toes to press her mouth to his. "I'll always want you, Jarrett, just as I want you now." Her voice was trembling. Did he realize what she was saying? What she wanted?

He took her hand and led her out of the music room, up the winding grand staircase as wide as Maggie's kitchen, and down the hallway toward the bedrooms.

"My room or one of the others?" Jarrett asked, stopping on the plush beige carpet.

"Yours." She rested her hand on his broad shoulders and kissed him with a longing she hadn't realized had existed inside her until this moment.

To hell with waiting for marriage, Maggie thought as Jarrett led her into his bedroom. *We may never marry. So many things could happen. There's so much against our making this work.*

But as she sat down on the edge of the single bed beside Jarrett, she realized she would never love a man as much as she loved this man. She wanted to give him something special, something that was hers to give to a man only once in her lifetime.

As Maggie and Jarrett began to make love, there was nothing awkward about their caresses. There was only inexperience.

Jarrett kissed her again and again until she melted into the softness of his down quilt, trembling in anticipation. She helped him take off his tux coat and bow tie. He unzipped her dress, kissing the length of her back as he drew the zipper down.

Maggie unbuttoned the gold studs of his white ruffled shirt one button at a time, feeling his warm skin under her palm.

The room was semidark, with only the hall light to illuminate the bed. She watched his facial expressions change, awed she could bring such a response from him.

As Jarrett unhooked her black bra, she shivered as much from desire as the coolness of the air.

"Maggie, Maggie," he whispered. They rolled on the bed, touching, exploring. Every kiss seemed right to Maggie, every caress.

Finally she helped him remove her hose and panties. Jarrett slipped out of his black trousers, then his white briefs. As he slipped under the sheet beside her, she laid back, her head on his pillow.

"We don't have to do this if you don't want to," he whispered in her ear, rolling over until his body covered hers. "We could just hold each other."

Maggie lifted her hips to meet his. It was instinct. The feel of his stiff, warm penis against her leg made her tremble. She was so hot inside she felt she was going to explode. Her breath came short and shallow. Sweat beaded above her upper lip. "I want to," she whispered. "I've wanted to for months."

Jarrett kissed her breast, teasing her nipple into a stiff peak. "All right, but if you want to stop, you tell me."

She smiled at his words, knowing he meant what he said . . . knowing she could trust him.

Jarrett rolled off her and reached into the drawer of his nightstand, fumbling for something. A rubber, she hoped.

"Got it," he whispered.

In the semidarkness, Maggie watched with fascination as he tried to roll the contraption on.

"Jarrett?"

"Um-hm?"

"Have . . . have you done this before?"

"This?" He tossed the foil package, making light of the inept moment.

"No." She rubbed his bare shoulder. "This."

"Oh. You mean *this*." Ready, he rolled on top of her again.

"Right, *this*," she whispered, looking up at him. "With . . . with another girl, I mean."

"Well, sure. I . . . just a couple of times."

Maggie couldn't help feeling a little disappointed. But she pushed the emotion aside, trying to be mature. Jarrett was older than she was, an attractive male. Of course he'd been with other girls.

"Just three or four," Jarrett went on quickly. "But that was before I met you." He kissed her cheek. "So don't worry." He nibbled her ear lobe. "I know what I'm doing."

Maggie relaxed. What did she care about the others? Jarrett was hers now. She let her thoughts go, allowing her physical body to take over. He felt so good lying on top of her, kissing her, touching her, whispering her name.

As he finally pushed inside her, it wasn't what Maggie had expected. Maybe she'd been watching too much TV, reading too many books. There was no pain, but there was no moaning ecstasy, either. It just felt good.

Maggie clung to Jarrett as he moved inside her. He whispered her name in her ear, panting. He told her he loved her.

It was over pretty quickly. She heard him groan and then he went slack, dropping his full weight on top of her. He rolled off her and onto the bed, his face covered with a thin sheen of sweat. He slipped out of the bed and went to the bathroom, coming back a minute later.

Jarrett lifted the sheet and slid into the single bed beside her. He pulled her into his arms. For the first time, Maggie felt awkward. Her heart was still racing. Jarrett kissed her temple and lay back against the pillow.

Maggie stroked the slippery pillowcase. "Satin sheets? Pretty fancy. If I didn't know better, Jarrett McKay, I'd think you planned the evening to lead to this."

She saw his grin in the darkness. "Well . . ."

"Yes?"

"I . . . I admit I was hoping."

She laughed. She didn't mind. It was what they had both wanted. "It's OK," she whispered, kissing his mouth.

"But, Maggie."

"Mmm-hmmm?" She rested her head on his pillow, feeling like an old married lady already.

"I, uh, I didn't exactly tell the truth when I said I'd done this three or four times before."

She raised up on her elbow to look at him. His blond hair was mussed, his blue eyes reflecting guilt. "What? You've done it a hundred times?"

He laughed nervously. "No. Actually, I was a virgin. I . . . I just didn't want you to think I didn't know what I was doing."

"Jarrett!" She pulled the pillow out from under his head and hit him with it. "I can't believe you lied to me." But inside, she was pleased.

"Sorry." He slipped the pillow back under his head

and patted it, indicating she should lie down. "But anyway, it'll be better next time. For you. I promise."

Maggie laughed and kissed him, understanding he was talking about her having an orgasm. It was funny how they could make love, but they couldn't talk about it yet. "I do love you, Jarrett. And I will marry you."

He propped himself up on his elbow so they were facing each other, their young, naked bodies pressing together. "So it's official. We're engaged." Then he paused. "But I don't think we should say anything to anyone yet. They wouldn't understand. Especially with me going to school in Spain next year."

She was trying not to think about his year abroad. It had been arranged before they started dating. Even though he said he'd cancel the trip, Maggie thought it was important that he go. "I agree. We won't tell anyone. My mom would have a cow."

He grinned. "Mine would, too."

Maggie looked into his deep blue eyes, lost in his love. "But we won't let them come between us, will we? Not them, not Spain."

"Nothing could come between us, Maggie," Jarrett answered sincerely, "because I love you and you love me. That's all that matters."

They kissed again, sealing their promise. Maggie pulled back and looked at him, her eyes filled with mischief. "So, want to try it again?"

Jarrett fell back onto the pillow, pulling her into his arms, and their laughter mingled until it was a single voice.

* * *

Five Months Later

Jarrett tipped his head back and chugged his fifth beer. He missed Maggie. The party wasn't any fun without her, even if it was in his honor. All his friends from Belltown were giving him this going away party. Next week he'd be headed off for a tour of Europe and then on to Spain, where he'd be meeting his host family in Madrid.

Maggie hadn't been able to come to his party here at the sandpits, where he and his friends had hung out when they were still in high school. Somehow her Mom had found out about it and she'd been forbidden to go. " 'Dangerous,' " Maggie had imitated her mom over the phone. " 'Beer. Boys. Girls. Nothing but trouble. Somebody will drown. The cops'll show up. That or you'll get knocked up.' "

Jarrett and Maggie had laughed at the last statement. They'd been so careful since Christmas. He always used rubbers and they'd even talked about her getting on the pill just to be extra cautious—not that he wouldn't want their baby if she got pregnant. Not that he wouldn't take care of them, marry her and be the father of their child. But Jarrett didn't want anything getting in the way of her becoming a doctor. She wanted it too much. He wanted it for her.

In the end, they'd decided since he'd be gone almost a whole year, only returning for Christmas, they would go ahead with the condoms and she'd start taking the pill when he came home for good.

Jarrett took the last swallow of his beer and tossed

the empty bottle into the back of Zach's red pickup. Somebody pushed another into his hand.

Hard rock blared from a boombox on the roof of Zach's truck. He watched with detached interest as some girl dancing on the edge of the sandpit fell in, screaming as she went over the side into the water. Several guys standing around sucking down beers laughed and clapped their hands. Some jumped in with her.

"So what do you think of your party?" Zach whacked him on the back. Even in the dim moonlight, Jarrett could tell his friend was wasted.

Jarrett nodded, leaning on the fender of the pickup "Not bad." He glanced behind him. "So where'd the girls come from? Friends of yours?" The carload had pulled up about half an hour ago. They were rough looking, with dyed hair. Some were tattooed. All of them were wearing short cutoffs and skintight tees that showed off more than they covered. Party girls.

"Nah." Zach sipped his beer. "Crashers." He shrugged. "But what the hell. They brought more beer and we might get lucky, right?" He elbowed his best buddy.

Jarrett grinned with Zach, but the thought of being with a girl other than Maggie didn't appeal to him. He loved her. He'd made a commitment for the rest of his life, he hoped. He wouldn't want Maggie to be with anyone else, so that meant he had to keep his own dick in his pants, didn't it?

"I thought you and Jill were getting serious," Jarrett said.

"Yeah, we are. Or, rather, *she* is."

"And she doesn't mind your messing around?"

Zach looked at Jarrett as if he'd grown another head. "Are you crazy? She'd have my balls in a nutcracker if she caught me." He winked. "So I just have to be careful I don't get caught, eh?"

Jarrett watched Zach saunter off, weaving and bobbing in his drunkenness. Maybe he'd just wait a while till his beers wore off and head for home. These guys wouldn't even notice he was gone, as drunk as they were.

"Hey, how about a shot of tequila?"

Jarrett looked up from his beer to see a girl throw her leg up on the bumper of the truck. She was tall, though not as tall as Maggie, a thin girl with bleached white hair cut short and spiky. She had a pretty smile, but her eye makeup was so heavy she looked like a prizefighter. Jarrett preferred the way Maggie did her face; he could barely tell she wore makeup at all.

The girl waved a bottle at him. "You up for it, big guy?"

Jarrett wrinkled his nose. It was hard not to stare at her small, braless tits under her tight black tank top. Just because he and Maggie were engaged didn't mean he wasn't as horny as the other guys. So long as he didn't act on it. "I don't know. I'm not really into tequila."

"Ah, come on. Just one? Got a saltshaker and a lime." She held up her hand. "Just a little taste?"

Jarrett exhaled. He'd had just enough beer not to be thinking clearly. "What the hell. Why not?"

"Atta boy."

The blond poured him a shot into a Tupperware cup,

and he drank it in one swallow. He couldn't help grimacing as it went down. It tasted like paint thinner smelled.

She laughed, rubbing his arm with her breast as she reached for the cup. "The next one goes down better, I promise."

She poured herself a shot, salting the lime and then licking it before she downed the drink. "Wow." She smacked her red lips. "Good." She grinned, wiggling her butt down beside him on the tailgate. "Another?"

He was already feeling the effects of the straight alcohol. His head was buzzing "Maybe in a minute." Talk about horny—she kept touching him. First she just touched his bare arm. Then she rested her hand on his thigh. Jarrett knew he ought to leave before he got into trouble. He kept thinking he'd stay just another minute and then join the other guys.

They shared another shot, and after she swallowed hers, she surprised him by pressing her tequila-wet lips to his. "How about a little something else?"

She whispered in his ear and Jarrett knew he must have blushed. Thank God it was dark out. He'd have been embarrassed otherwise. Now he didn't know what to do. He couldn't think clearly. She tasted different than Maggie. Her kiss was harder. She smelled different, too. Her perfume was heavy, musky.

"That's quite the invitation." He tried to sound cool. Right now he was just hoping he wasn't going to fall off the bumper onto his ass. "Especially coming from someone whose name I don't even know."

She got up off the bumper and straddled his knees, climbing onto his lap. Jarrett didn't know what to do.

He'd never had a girl come on to him like this before. He kind of liked it.

"Lisa," she purred.

She was right in his face, her little tits pressed against his T-shirt. Her fingers brushed the crotch of his blue jeans. Against his will, he was getting a hard on. "Oh, Lisa? Lisa what?"

She lifted her shoulder and stared him straight in the eye. Her breath smelled of cigarette smoke and tequila. "Who gives a fat rat's ass? All I want to know, big guy, is if you're ready for a good time?"

FIVE

The Present

Maggie stumbled to the bathroom, flipped on the light, and used the toilet. She wasn't due at the hospital until seven a.m., but she liked to get in early, have a cup of coffee, and get her head straight before her day began. She'd been offered a leave of absence for bereavement, but she'd refused.

She needed to work right now. She needed to order X rays and to suture, to call for consults, to follow as humdrum a routine as possible. She needed to keep from thinking about babies and coffins, about her little Jordan and the incomprehensible thought that she would never hold him in her arms again, would never smell his cookie breath or feel his duck-down hair against her chin.

Maggie groaned and leaned against the sink, staring into the oval antique mirror. God. She looked like Frankenstein's Bride. Her hair stuck out in spikes, her skin was pale and splotchy, and her eyes were red and puffy from all the crying last night.

"Perfect," she murmured, reaching for her contact case. "I'll be scaring off my patients with this mug."

After putting her contacts in so she could find the kitchen, she shrugged into a terry robe hanging on the back of the bathroom door and went down hall. The coffeepot was already making chugging, spewing sounds as it spit out her morning dose of caffeine.

She poured a cup and went to the adjacent living room, drew open the curtains, and curled up on the leather couch she'd bought just for this spot. Here in her second-story living room, she could peer over the dunes and watch the sun come up. It was her own piece of heaven on earth—or so she had thought until two weeks ago.

Maggie drew her bare feet under her and sipped her black coffee. She swallowed the bitter brew, though she didn't even like coffee. She'd started drinking it when she began sleeping with Stanley. He thought it silly to make tea and coffee every morning, so he'd tossed out her old teakettle from her undergrad days. He bought a fancy new appliance that could be programmed to make coffee in the morning, tell the time, and, hell, maybe even set the VCR, she didn't know.

She took another sip of the coffee, irritated. "You shouldn't have thrown out my kettle," she said aloud. "You knew I liked it, even if it was yard sale and had a broken handle."

The moment the words came out of her mouth she was ashamed. Stanley was dead, for God's sake. How could she be angry over a teakettle?

But she *was* angry. She was angry with Stanley for all the ways he had managed her life. She was angry with herself for letting him. She was angry with him for leaving her, dumping all that crap back in her lap. Most of all, she was angry with God for taking Stanley and her baby away and leaving her with nothing.

She went back into the kitchen, dumped the coffee into the sink, and chose a small saucepan from the rack over the island. She filled it with water and put it on the stove to heat. She knew she had loose tea and a strainer somewhere. She kept them around the house for Kyle. He wouldn't drink coffee from Stanley's coffeemaker.

"I like tea," she said aloud, glad she'd built the more costly single-family dwelling and not the town house Stanley had suggested was a better investment. This way no one could hear her ranting as she slowly went stark raving mad so early in the morning.

"Don't like coffee. Don't like it, Stanley. I told you that, told you a hundred times, you stupid son of a bitch. I don't like ketchup on my hot dogs, either."

She slammed the tea tin on the counter, then the strainer. Somehow slamming things—hearing the sound, feeling the resistance—made her feel better. She dumped some of the tea directly into the simmering water.

"If you'd just listened to me once in a while, if I'd made you listen," she said, tapping her bare foot as she waited for the water to boil.

If . . . then what? What was she saying? She wasn't making any sense. She really was going crazy.

She fought the hot tears welling in her eyes. She couldn't keep crying like this. She couldn't cry for the rest of her life.

She reached for a clean mug in the cabinet and her fingers brushed a sippy cup with a lid on it. *Jordan's.*

She smiled and swallowed the lump in her throat. "Oh, Jordy," she whispered. "My sweet one."

She popped the lid off and, using the strainer, poured some tea. The plastic cup was hot on her fingers, but she didn't care. It was Jordan's. His hands had once held this cup, his little mouth had touched the rim of it. Feeling a strange sense of comfort in the thought, she returned to the couch. The sky was just beginning to brighten with the light of dawn.

Another day.

And now what? What did she have to get up for now? What reason did she have to ever want to see the sun rise again?

Jordan was gone.

Good old Stanley was gone.

But still the sun rose.

The thought of the other baby popped into her head out of nowhere. She hardly ever thought of that baby— her daughter, the baby girl she'd borne when other girls her age were midway though the first semester of their freshman year of college.

Maggie closed her eyes and tried to remember the baby. But all she could see was Jordan, all pink and wrinkled, with gonads the size of walnuts. She hadn't actually seen more than a glimpse of the first baby. She'd been drugged for the birth. It had all been a haze of blurred sights and strange sounds, as if it hadn't happened to her, but to someone else. Yet it was true. It was all true. At the age of eighteen, she had given birth to a daughter. Jarrett's daughter.

Maggie closed her eyes, cradling the blue Tupperware sippy cup as memories flooded her. She never had a chance to tell Jarrett. The cheating son of a bitch had confessed he'd had sex with Lisa, and Maggie had broken up with him. He'd gone off to Spain. A few weeks later, she had realized she was pregnant—the typical story of young love gone wrong. She'd forgiven Lisa years ago. It was too much work to hold the grudge. But she hadn't forgiven Jarrett. She'd held onto that betrayal stubbornly. It was his fault she'd lost her baby.

The telephone rang, and Maggie reached for the cordless handset. She didn't wonder who was calling her at dawn. She knew.

"Kyle." She sipped tea from her sippy cup.

"Maggie."

"How'd you know I wasn't asleep? You could have wakened me."

"I know better." His sleepy voice was comforting. "I was just calling to say good morning before you slipped off to work."

"Liar. You were calling to see if I'd OD'd or something."

"Did you?"

"Yup." She finished her tea and left the cup on the antique farm table behind the couch, then padded barefoot to her bedroom to find clothes. "Ibuprofen. 500 milligrams. Cramps like a bitch."

"The joy of womanhood," he teased.

She gave a little laugh that came out thick. There would be no more joy of womanhood out of her womb. It was practically nonfunctioning, thick with non-life-sustaining tissue. Dead like her babies.

When she didn't comment, he picked up the conversation for her. "What're you doing?"

"Finding clothes. Going to take a shower and head off."

"What to wear," he sighed. "The white slacks and lab coat or the white slacks and lab coat?"

She pulled a pair of white cotton uniform pants out of the closet and yanked off the plastic dry cleaner's bag. Remnants of Stanley. "I was thinking I'd go with the white slacks and white lab coat."

"Tonal. I like tonal."

Their conversation was utterly frivolous, and yet it was Kyle's superficial conversation that had been keeping her from shattering these last two weeks. He knew how fragile she was right now and how to handle her.

"How about lunch today?"

She went to the bathroom and turned on both showerheads. "Right, me with time for lunch. By midmorning, our vacationers will have awakened from their drunken slumber. They'll be out cutting their bare feet on poptops, frying their skin on the beach, and throwing their backs out on boogie boards. I don't think so."

"A girl's got to eat," he chastised.

She dropped her robe, her panties, and her T-shirt on the bathroom floor. "Cafeteria food suit you?"

"I'll pack," he said dryly. "One?"

"Ish."

"Ciao."

She smiled, thankful for his friendship. *"Adios."*

She hit the off button on her phone, left it on the sink, and stepped into the shower. The steamy water beat rhythmically on her bare back and she mentally switched gears. She'd think about work now, about the hospital and her patients. She'd table her tragedy, neatly placing it in a separate compartment in her mind. She'd table the past and the thoughts of the baby she'd never held in her arms. It was the only way she could deal with her son's and husband's deaths right now. It was the only way she could go on.

"Kyle." Maggie folded a piece of romaine lettuce into her whole wheat roll and took a bite of the veggie and cheese sandwich he'd brought her from the deli. "Did I ever tell you I had a baby before Jordan?"

He choked on his tuna salad. "B-baby." He wiped his mouth with a white napkin he'd brought from the deli.

They were eating in the physicians' lounge, empty except for them. Most of Maggie's colleagues were still steering clear of her. When people didn't know what to say, she found they preferred to say nothing at all. In fact, they preferred to pretend victims of such tragedies as hers didn't exist at all, as if she had died, too.

"No," Kyle said when he found his voice. "No, I don't recall your saying you'd had another baby, Maggie dear. Must have slipped your mind."

She put down the sandwich. It tasted like sawdust anyway. "I didn't tell you because, honestly, I never thought much about it. It was one of the things in the past that I just kind of chose to forget."

He reached for his diet soda. "I take it you want to tell me now?"

Without preface, she gave him a brief account of the

whole sordid affair with an emotional distance that frightened her. She hadn't realized how raw the wound was until now—now that Jordan was dead.

She ended the story and sat staring at her sandwich.

Kyle spoke without a tone of judgment in his voice. "So where is she?"

She watched him move his hand as if he wanted to take hers, then pull it back. He knew if he touched her she might fall from the cliff's edge she teetered on.

"I don't know," she said simply.

The door to the lounge opened and one of the other ER physicians walked in and stopped short at the sight of Maggie. For a second she thought he might turn around and hightail it out. Instead he nodded, grunted a greeting, and made a beeline for the coffeepot. He was out in under a minute.

Kyle waited until the door closed behind him. "You want to know where she is?"

She opened her hands, staring at the sandwich in front of her. "In the past, I always thought I didn't. She's adopted, has a mother and a father who love her. Brothers and sisters. I just want to know she's all right."

He studied her face. "You just want to know? This isn't some crazy grief-induced idea of finding your long lost daughter and suing for custody, ripping her out of the only home she's ever known, from the arms of the only parents she's ever known?"

Maggie rose from her wobbly chair, crushing the half-eaten sandwich in her napkin. "You're brutal."

"Truthful."

She walked toward the garbage can. "I just want to

know where she is. I don't even know that I would try and contact her . . . family." She glanced at him. "I just want to know."

Having apparently lost his appetite, too, Kyle neatly rolled his sandwich in its paper and placed it in the brown bag to eat later. He rose from the chair, looking completely out of place in his Calvin Klein suit in the shabby lounge. "You could be opening a bag of worms here, Maggie love. You might think this could be cathartic, but it could be devastating."

She eyed him. "I'm a strong woman."

"I know you are. But even the strongest can only take so much. You find her, *if* you find her, and it could be like losing her all over again."

When he said those words, she realized her mind was already made up. "I've needed to do this for a long time." She folded her arms around her waist. "Put the whole thing with Jarrett to rest as I should have before Stanley."

He nodded, and she was thankful he understood. Having voiced her desire to know about her daughter, she realized she feared her teenage affair with Jarrett McKay and the illegitimate baby that union had produced had come between her and Stanley. She knew by Kyle's expression he understood she felt guilty as hell about it. He understood her need to forgive herself.

"I suppose doing a little research would give you something to do," he said. "Something else to think about."

She leaned against the counter. "Beats sedation."

He walked over to her and kissed her on the cheek. "Go for it, toots."

She lifted her gaze to meet his with a new sense of hope. Hope for what, she didn't know, but it was buoying just the same. "Thanks."

"Let me know what you find out. I've got a lawyer friend who might be able to help you if need be."

"Friend?" She lifted an eyebrow.

He shrugged. "Hoping for more, but just a friend right now."

"Thanks for the lunch," Maggie called as Kyle stepped into the hall.

"Sure. Next time maybe you'll eat it."

She was almost smiling when the door closed behind him.

SIX

"I certainly understand that, Mrs. Baker." Maggie tapped her pen on the ink blotter on her desk, trying unsuccessfully not to sound terse. After all, the woman was just doing her job. "I'm not interested in invading anyone's privacy. I'm simply trying to—"

The hospital administrator in Tucson interrupted her again. This time Maggie heard the woman's voice, but she didn't really absorb what she was saying. The answer was clear. It didn't matter that Maggie had been the one who gave birth to the baby. Maggie had given the baby up for adoption. According to Mrs. Baker, Maggie had signed the adoption release. She no longer had any rights.

Before Mrs. Baker could offer her apology for being unable to give her any further assistance, Maggie cut the conversation short. "Thank you for your help," she said. "Have a fine day." She punched the off button on the cordless phone and dropped it on the eighteenth-century French writing desk.

Another dead end.

For two weeks, Maggie had been trying to get information about the baby she gave birth to fifteen years earlier on the seventeenth of November. So far, she'd hit nothing but obstacles and hadn't obtained one smidgen of information. Each hospital administrator she spoke to, each court representative, even the secretaries of private adoption agencies in the area, were quite sympathetic. They were also closemouthed, refusing to give Maggie any information.

Mrs. Baker, the administrator of the hospital since 1978, wouldn't even acknowledge Maggie had been a patient on the maternity ward or that private adoptions took place inside the walls of her domain. That information was confidential, protected by the Federal Privacy Act—so Mrs. Baker had repeated numerous times.

"Hell," Maggie muttered, covering her face with her hands.

"Things going that well?" Kyle entered the small office off her master bedroom, carrying a tray with a pot of tea and a plate of pastries that smelled delicious.

"Earl Grey and walnut scones," he announced. Without asking, he poured her a cup and served her two flaky triangles of pastry on a turn-of-the-century flowered plate.

"Pull up a chair." She reached for the tea. She'd been living on Kyle's tea and breads since the accident. It was the only thing she could keep down.

"Don't mind if I do." He slid a leather armchair across the hardwood floor to the front of the desk and made himself a cup of tea.

"You don't have to keep coming over here and making me food," she said, relieved that he did.

"It's not for you, dear. You're just an excuse to use

that fancy oven of yours." He licked the crumbs from his fingers. "So how goes the baby search?"

"It goes not," she said glumly. "No one will tell me anything. It's as if I imagined the whole thing. I can't even get the hospital to admit I was there."

He eyed her over the brim of his teacup. "Thought about asking your mother if she could remember anything? You said she took care of the paperwork."

"Cold day in bloody hell," she snapped.

He sat back quietly in his chair and sipped his tea.

She waited for her blind fury to pass before she spoke. "I'm sorry," she said softly, genuinely so. "I'm not angry with you. I'm angry with her, with myself."

"You were a baby yourself." He didn't make the statement as an excuse, only as truth.

"You're right. I was." She traced the gold filigree paint that rimmed her teacup and sighed heavily. "Anyway, I don't think I can discuss it with Mother. I know it doesn't make sense, but I just can't do it. It hurts too much. We've never spoken of the matter. Not one word has ever passed between us. I don't know that it ever will."

"Not even if you find your daughter?"

"I don't know," she answered.

He cradled his teacup thoughtfully. "Maggie, are you sure you really want this information?"

She glanced up in surprise. "Of course I do."

"It hasn't just been a way to keep your mind off Stanley and Jordan?"

She swallowed a mouthful of warm tea, giving his suggestion careful consideration before she answered him. "It has, but it isn't. I told you, I should have done this years ago. I threw myself into my studies and then into my career to get away from the whole mess. But I was kidding myself to think I could go the rest of my life pretending it never happened."

There was a long, quiet pause, giving them both time to think, before he spoke again. "Tell me something. If we . . . you do locate your daughter, what are you going to do then? Have you thought about that?"

She had. "I intend to contact her parents, tell them who I am and where they can reach me. Kyle"—she leaned across the desk—"she's fourteen years old now, almost fifteen. She's *got* to be asking questions about me, wondering who I am, why I gave her away."

"*If* her parents have told her she's adopted."

She set her cup down hard on the blotter and tea spilled into the saucer. "You're certainly being Mr. Supportive."

"I'm playing devil's advocate." He reached for another scone. "It's my job."

A few notes of a Jimmy Buffett tune played in her head and she had to smile. Kyle was right. It *was* his job to keep her in line, to keep her thinking reasonably.

She met his gaze. "I have to try. Can you understand that? Even if they turn me away cold. At least then, if she ever tries to find me later, I'll be able to tell her I attempted to contact her. She'll know I cared about her." She nibbled on the scone. Food was actually beginning to have taste again. "It happens all the time, you know. Women adopted as babies grow up, have children of their own, and feel a part of their life is missing. They track down their mothers and are reunited."

"With mothers who are doing ten to twenty in the state pen."

She grimaced. "Very funny. I'm not in the state pen, at least not yet. And I'm not the kind of mother a teenage girl would be ashamed of."

"But you're not her mother, Maggie dear," he said softly. "Not anymore."

She stared into the amber liquid of her teacup. His words cut her to the quick. But he was right, damn him. He was right. She stood, pressing her hands on her desk. "Want to go for a walk on the beach?" All of a sudden the room felt stuffy. She felt hemmed in.

"Sure."

They started down the beach, walking north. Though it was a Tuesday morning, the beach was already beginning to fill with vacationers hoping to catch a few extra hours of the sun's brutal rays.

They walked side by side for two blocks before Maggie spoke again. "I understand what you're saying about my not being her mother. I really do. I didn't change her diapers, nurse her through the chicken pox, or watch her in the school Christmas play." She struggled to keep the emotion out of her voice. "But she came from my body, Kyle. You can't imagine what that's like."

"No, I can't imagine, and I won't pretend I do." He took her hand and squeezed it. "I just don't want you to set yourself up for a fall. I don't want you hurt any more than you already are."

She nodded, appreciating the feel of another's touch. She missed the feel of Jordan's little hand in hers. She even missed the feel of Stanley's arm draped casually over her shoulder. She felt so alone.

"I'm not saying it won't hurt. I just feel as if this is a part of life I need to settle before I can go on."

Maggie halted along the outgoing shoreline to watch a young girl with reddish-blond hair kneeling in the sand. She was building a sandcastle on the edge of the surf, a whole bucket full of serious sandcastle tools at her side. A pair of sunglasses worn like a headband held her hair out of her face. She had to be a local.

"Think she's fourteen?" Maggie asked softly, not really looking for answer. "Probably not." She chuckled. "No fluorescent blue eye shadow or headphone attached to her head."

"Come on." Kyle tugged on her hand, turning her back they way they'd come. "Got time to meet someone?"

She turned away from the girl. "Who?"

"An old friend. He runs a pottery shop on the avenue."

"I don't need any pottery right now."

"He sells pottery for a living, but he's a real computer geek. A superior hacker, I've heard."

She halted. Cold water ran over her bare feet. "A computer hacker? What do I want with a computer hacker?"

He lifted one shoulder and his neatly ironed yellow polo shirt rippled. "Surely there are hospital records. You just need access to them."

Maggie's eyes widened. "Kyle Dickerson! That's illegal."

"So you're not interested?"

"Of course I am." She released his hand and took off down the beach, calling over her shoulder. "Race you to the car!"

"Taylor!" Jarrett McKay leaned on the rail of the living room deck of his parent's beach house and studied the beach. He cupped his hands around his mouth and hollered again. "Taylor!"

"I'm coming. I'm coming!" He heard his daughter's voice rise from somewhere below the deck.

The outside shower came on, then turned off. A minute later his daughter appeared in denim shorts and a T-shirt, barefooted, her hair tousled. Perched on her freckled nose were a pair of very chic black cat's-eye sunglasses. "You should come down and see the castle I made, Dad." She pushed the glasses up on the bridge of her nose. "It's got turrets and everything."

He glanced out over the dunes toward the ocean. "Tide coming in?"

She frowned. "Going out. You don't think I'd spend an hour on a castle if the tide was coming in, do you?"

He grinned. Miss Logical. Miss Efficient. That was his Taylor. "How about you come back in and help me unpack for a while? Then we'll go down and see it together. Deal?"

"We couldn't do it now?"

"No whining. You know how I feel about whiny female voices." He hooked a thumb in the direction of the living room that was in utter chaos, even for his living room. "First work, then play."

Taylor groaned. "Work, work, work, that's all I do

is work." She tossed her shoulder-length strawberry-blond hair in an exaggerated gesture. "I'm nothing but a Cinderella to you."

"Grab a box from the truck on your way up, Cindy."

Jarrett returned to the living room, not wanting to hear his daughter's reply. His parents had warned him it wouldn't be easy raising a girl once she was a teenager, but they didn't know the half of it.

With a sigh, Jarrett paused in the middle of the living room that overlooked the ocean. Last year he had purchased the house from his parents, who had moved to Florida. Then, after much soul-searching, he had decided to move from Philadelphia to the Delaware beach town and get settled before the school year began.

In the fall, Taylor would be starting her sophomore year of high school, and a public school in Delaware was more suited to his daughter's needs and personality than the private high school she would have attended in Philadelphia. Besides, both of them were happier here at the beach than in the city. It was quieter, at least through the school year, and the lifestyle was less hectic. Jarrett and Taylor had always spent summers here, even when she was a baby, but it had been both their dreams to take up residence permanently in the little town of Talbany Beach.

Jarrett knew he was fortunate to have a job that allowed him to work anywhere. It was one of the advantages of being a small business owner. He'd have to make bimonthly trips to his main office in Philadelphia, but most of the work could be handled from here by means of his computer, a fax, and the extra phone line he'd already had installed.

"Where do you want this?" Taylor appeared at the top of the stairs, her face blocked by a huge cardboard moving box.

"What does it say?"

"Kitchen."

"Then my guess would be—"

"The kitchen," she laughed.

He chuckled over her silliness with her. He and Taylor had their battles. She was stubborn, still immature at times, and she a flair for dramatics. But she was a good kid, bright, articulate. She didn't smoke or drink and she came home on time. She was a straight A student with a love of history, especially anything medieval. He was dammed proud of her and loved her fiercely. Being a single parent wasn't easy, but he had never regretted his decision, not once in all these years.

"God's teeth, Dad. This thing is heavy." She dropped the box onto the counter. "What have you got in it?"

He grabbed one end of a bookcase standing in the center of the room and began to drag it across the carpet to a wall. Halfway across the room, one end came off, but he shoved it back on—another one of his projects that hadn't quite gone together as it should have. "I don't know. Open it. Check inside." He pushed the shaky bookcase against the wall and located a box marked "books." "Put it away, while you're at it."

She picked up a utility knife from the counter and cut open the box. "Hey, Dad."

He sat on the floor, cross-legged. "Hey, Taylor."

"Dad, what was she like?"

He didn't have to ask who *she* was. He knew who she meant. It seemed as if ever since Taylor had turned into a teen she'd been obsessed with her mother. "What do you mean? I've told you, Taylor. She was pretty. She was smart. She was fun. She was just like you."

"Pretty!" she scoffed. "That doesn't tell me anything. Pretty like cute? Pretty like a classic Greek goddess? A Katharine Hepburn? I don't understand why you don't have any pictures of her. That's the most ridiculous thing I've ever heard of, not having pictures of your wife. When I grow up and get married, I'm going to make my husband take pictures of me. That way if die, they'll know what *I* looked like."

He let her rattle on because it was the easiest thing to do. By trial and error, he'd discovered that allowing her to ramble until she ran out of steam was the quickest to way to move on, leaving the subject behind.

Jarrett didn't like talking about her mother. He didn't even like thinking about her, but for Taylor's sake he knew he had to keep his feelings hidden from her. There was no need for Taylor to know any of the sordid truth about her mother. She had been pretty and smart and fun, and that was the memory he wanted Taylor to carry with her always.

"Of course when *I* get married," Taylor continued as she placed mismatched fast-food glasses in the cupboard beside the sink, "I'm not going to have one child. I think it's a sin to have only one child." She placed her hand dramatically on her breast. "A burden too heavy for some children to bear."

He hid a smile of amusement as he sat cross-legged on the floor and shoved books into the bookshelf. His laughter would only encourage her.

"One box down," she said as she tossed the empty

box into a pile in the corner of the living room. She placed her hands on her narrow hips and rolled her eyes as she surveyed the room. "And only a hundred zillion or so to go."

"So what are you waiting for?" He reached for another armful of books. "Grab another box."

SEVEN

Maggie drove down the avenue where Kyle's men's clothing store was located, searching frantically for a parking space. Someone pulled out in front of her, and she hit her horn.

"Come on, come on," she murmured. "There's got to be one space. One lousy parking space."

She'd already passed his shop twice, riding up the avenue to the ocean boardwalk and looping back around again. Every parking space was taken by vacationers trying to cram in a little shopping while still getting time on the beach. Maggie never came down the avenue during peak season unless it was to see Kyle. It was just too stressful.

She spotted backup lights on a vehicle three parking spaces ahead of her. Was someone leaving, or was the driver just resting his foot on the brake while he waited for passengers to unload? "Please, please," she whispered. "Please be going home."

She had to get to Kyle's shop. In less than a week, his hacker friend had found information on a private adoption that took place in Tucson on the day in question. But Kyle wanted to tell her what had been discovered in person, not on the phone. He had wanted to wait until tonight over dinner, but she was working. She had to know now.

The line of cars eased slowly ahead of her. She flipped on her right blinker. *What luck,* she thought optimistically, still not knowing for sure she would get the space. *Only a block from Kyle's shop.*

The driver of the car in front of her, a woody station wagon with Pennsylvania plates and beach chairs tied to the luggage rack, braked suddenly and came to a stop.

"What now?" she murmured. "You can't just stop here." She lifted her hands off the wheel. "You can't stop in the middle of the street."

A chubby teen walked between two parked cars, carrying drinks and a bucket of fries. The car was apparently waiting for him and lunch.

She tapped on the leather steering wheel of her car. "Come on, come on." She glanced at her Timex. Stanley had bought her a beautiful Rolex, but it didn't have a second hand. What physician could work without a second hand, for pete's sake?

The rear door of the station wagon popped open and a Coke can tumbled out.

The driver behind Maggie laid on his car horn.

She gripped the wheel, glancing into her rearview mirror. "What do you want me to do? Drive over him?"

The teen passed the fries and drinks to someone inside the car. He went down on one knee to pick up the soda can.

Maggie turned the fan up on the air-conditioning and

a blast of cold air hit her in the face. If someone else took the parking space before she got into it, she didn't know what she'd do. Double park? Pull up on the sidewalk? She was beyond reason now.

She watched the teen hitch up his sagging knee-length surf shorts and stand, can in hand. "Good boy," she congratulated. "Littering is bad. Awful. *Now get in the flippin' car!"*

She stared at the still empty parking space just beyond her grasp. The brass ring.

The boy jumped into the back seat. The wagon rolled forward and Maggie eased her green Jag into the parking space.

She leaped out of the car, taking a handful of quarters with her. She dropped two into the meter. Slinging her purse over her shoulder she took off down the sidewalk, dodging strollers and sunburned couples walking hand in hand, window shopping.

This is it, she thought. *He has something. Kyle knows where I can find my daughter. This is it!*

She was so scared she was afraid she was going to pee her pants.

"Kyle!" Maggie burst into Black Tie White Polo and rushed past a mannequin wearing a white tennis sweater and tasteful navy shorts and holding a tennis racket.

She spotted Kyle near a display of dress socks. He held up one finger. He was with a customer.

She took a deep breath and walked to the counter. An elderly gentleman, one of Kyle's employees, Mr. Rolfson, was ringing up a tie with sand buckets on it for another customer.

"Afternoon, Mr. Rolfson."

Her heart pounded in her chest. Despite the chill in the store, her palms and the back of her neck were sweaty.

"Dr. Turner. So sorry to hear of your loss," the gray-haired gentleman said kindly.

She smiled hesitantly. The condolences were still hard, but they were getting easier. At least she wasn't bursting into tears in public now. "Thank you. I appreciate it."

Kyle approached the counter, carrying two pairs of socks, two shirts, and a tie. "Tony, would you ring this up for me?" He glanced at Maggie. "Maggie and I will be in the back."

"Sure thing."

Kyle laid the items on the tasteful wood counter and spoke to his customer. "Thanks so much for stopping by. Mr. Rolfson will ring you up."

Maggie followed Kyle beyond the curtain behind the counter to his small office off the storeroom. He was dressed casually today in khakis, loafers, and a plaid polo shirt, but, as always, he looked as if he'd just stepped off the pages of a men's fashion magazine.

"What have you got? What did he find out?" She practically jumped up and down.

He waited until she stepped over the threshold of his office and closed the door behind her. For the first time since she'd entered his shop, she saw concern etched on his face. Concern for her.

Crap. What now? she thought. "What is it?"

"You should sit down." He indicated the chair at his desk. The office was compact but neat, just like Kyle.

"I don't want to sit down," she said testily. "I want to know what you found out. I've been waiting fourteen years, Kyle."

He ran his hand through his stylishly moussed hair. "This is probably a mistake on my part."

She dropped her crocheted purse on his desk. She was sweating heavily now, despite the light cotton white T-shirt and pants she wore. She intended to go directly to the hospital from here. "Kyle . . ." She begged him with her gaze.

"All right. All right." He reached for a sheet of paper that lay on his desk, an ordinary piece of paper that Maggie knew would change her life forever.

"Thank you," she whispered. "Thank you so much."

"Thank me after you read it." He handed her the paper.

For a moment her vision was blurry. Did she really want to know? If she didn't, this was her opportunity to back down. Last chance.

I want to know.

She focused on the information sheet obviously printed from some legal file—printed illegally. It was dated exactly one week after Maggie gave birth in Tucson, and recorded in Baltimore, Maryland.

She scanned it quickly.

A request for temporary custody of a female child born in Tucson, adoption proceedings request forthcoming.

Her vision blurred again, this time from tears.

The request was signed and dated by Jarrett McKay.

* * *

"Bastard." Lisa leaned over the counter stirring her martini. It was eleven thirty in the morning—in her eyes, well within the acceptable time limits for drinking.

Maggie was drinking tea she'd brewed in the new Mrs. Tea she'd bought at the local supermarket. Lisa had come to visit for a few days to be with Maggie and help her sort out this mess her life had become.

"So you didn't know? Mother didn't tell you?"

"Mother never told me anything. Hell, I didn't even know why you'd gone to Aunt Sissy's until I figured it out myself and called you."

Maggie was still reeling in shock over the news that Jarrett was raising her daughter. Her daughter, her flesh-and-blood, was with him and not her. In all these years, she had never once suspected. It was almost too unbelievable to believe. Yet somewhere deep in her aching heart she knew it was true. *Aching, breaking heart*. Maggie nearly choked as she swallowed her tea. How had her life become a bad song?

Lisa went on, oblivious to the moisture Maggie brushed from her eyes. "And Mother—how could she give your baby away to Richie Rich? *Bitch.*"

"It was a private adoption, Lisa. She wouldn't have known who the baby went to."

"Well, someone sure as hell knew, whoever told the McKays to begin with. It had to be Mother."

Lisa said nothing of the fact that it was because of her that Maggie and Jarrett had broken up. Maggie couldn't help wondering if the event had meant so little to her that she had completely forgotten. But Maggie didn't bring it up. What would be the point?

"Lisa." Maggie tried to remain calm, in control of her emotions and the situation. It was the only way she could continue to function. "That's not fair. Mother would not have told the McKays I was pregnant."

Lisa laughed without humor as she poured her martini into a juice glass. "You just keep telling yourself that, sister. Whatever it takes to get you through the day."

Maggie followed Lisa into the living room. She didn't want to argue about their mother. It was a waste of time and precious energy. She wanted to talk about her daughter. Not about Jarrett, but about her baby. About what she should do next.

Lisa sat on the couch, propped her sandaled feet on the trunk that served as a coffee table, and stretched out her long, thin, tanning-bed tanned legs. She was dressed in white short shorts, a sleeveless blouse, and Italian white sandals. Maggie assessed that Lisa had probably paid as much for her casual ensemble as Maggie had paid for the leather couch.

"The question is, what should I do next?" She plopped down beside her sister in her running shorts and her torn Cornell Med School T-shirt.

"Do? Sue the bastard. Take your daughter and as much cash as you can get out of him. He's probably a hotshot lawyer." She glanced sideways at Maggie. "Wasn't he pre-law at Georgetown?"

"I haven't even found him yet." She sipped her tea from a salt-glazed mug. Right now she couldn't even imagine the encounter with Jarrett to come. "His parents sold their house. A neighbor said they'd moved to Tampa."

Lisa gave a snort and tipped her martini/juice glass. "Typical. What about Jarrett? Where did they say he went?"

"I didn't ask many questions. It was old Mr. Ferguson who lived next door to Jarrett. He knew more about the brother. Lives in LA, a psychologist, psychiatrist, something like that."

"Nothing on Richie?"

Maggie eyed her sister, surprised by the twinge she felt when Lisa cut on Jarrett. Lisa had never liked Jarrett. Even when she'd had sex with him, it hadn't been because it was Jarrett. A million other reasons, but not because she liked him. So why did Maggie care now what Lisa thought of him? He was the scum of the earth. Only scum would take a woman's child and never tell her. "Mr. Garrison said Mr. and Mrs. McKay didn't say much about Jarrett. It was all about his big brother and how he was a psychiatrist to the stars or some such nonsense."

"He didn't know where he lived? What he did for a living?"

"He thought he might be in Philly or Baltimore, but he couldn't remember. He *could,* however, remember what I wore to my senior prom." Maggie lifted an eyebrow, amused by the useless information.

"OK, so we start looking in Baltimore and Philadelphia."

Lisa got up and went back into the kitchen. Maggie listened to her make herself another martini. She really needed to talk to Lisa about her drinking again, but she would table that conversation for another time.

"Which city do you want? I'll take the other."

"Lisa, you don't have to do this. This is my problem. I can find him on my own. I'm sure you have better things to do than track down my old boyfriend."

"Track down my niece." Lisa stuck her head around the corner. "And what have I got better to do? Sit alone in my apartment and watch the home-shopping club? Wait for that wife-cheating, globe-hopping, son of a bitch of a husband of mine to pass through on his way to Japan? If I'm lucky I might get a nice dinner at a French restaurant or a reception at the White House." Her sarcasm was thick, her pain poorly hidden.

Maggie didn't understand why her sister married men like Ronald. He'd cheated on his wife to sleep with Lisa. What made her think it would be different once he married her? But, like the drinking, Maggie didn't want to get into the subject right now. What was the point? Lisa chose to live her life as she saw fit, and she was always quick to remind Maggie of that fact.

"It makes sense to check Baltimore first—don't you think? We could do it together." Maggie leaned over the back of the couch.

Lisa came out of the kitchen carrying her second martini. "Want to drive over, or do some legwork from here first?"

"It probably makes sense to check a phone book first for private and business listings," Maggie said.

"Sure, Miss Practical, but it would be more fun to go for the day. A person should have a little fun on her day off, you know. We could have a nice lunch." She regarded Maggie's clothes with a sniff. "Maybe do a little shopping. Pick you up a nice outfit or two."

"I don't need any clothes." Maggie responded a little more defensively than she intended. "What do I need clothes for? I wear uniforms to work. I run and sleep in this." She tugged on her T-shirt.

"Exactly." Lisa walked to the floor-to-ceiling windows that lined the east wall and gazed out at the breakers. "We've got to get you looking decent again, get you back into circulation."

Maggie knew it was coming. Lisa had been hinting over the phone for two weeks. It had been more than a month since the accident. Appropriate mourning time had passed, as far as her oversexed sister was concerned. Lisa thought Maggie ought to be out looking for dates, men to have wild sex with. The amusing thing was, Maggie had never had wild sex before, not with Stanley or anyone else. What made Lisa think she was going to now?

"I'll go for the lunch and we can shop for you, but I don't need anything. I don't want anything," Maggie finished firmly.

"Suit yourself." Lisa shrugged one thin shoulder. "But shopping always makes me feel better."

"Exactly." Maggie rose to go dress. "Makes *you* feel better. Not me." She started down the hall, then came back. "I need to go to Stanley's apartment, too. Think we should do that? I really should start cleaning it out."

Lisa glanced out the window again, finishing off her martini. "One biggie at a time, Maggie. Let's see if we

can find your daughter. Stanley's stuff isn't going anywhere."

Maggie nodded. Lisa was right. She'd already contacted a real estate agent, but he was showing the
apartment as it was. There was no hurry until they
had an interested buyer. She was just going to box
up everything and have the Salvation Army pick it
up. She would sell most of the furniture with the
apartment.

The only thing she really wanted was the antique
sleigh bed she and Stanley had bought together. She
had called it her wedding bed. He'd ended up putting
it, the smaller bed, in his apartment for practical reasons. She rarely slept in DC. He'd bought a king-size
bed for here, one they'd be more comfortable in together, he said. But secretly, practicality be damned,
she wished she'd kept the bed here at the beach.

"Maybe next time I get two days in a row off," Maggie said, "I could go to DC and you could help me
clean out the place." She glanced at her running shoes.
"I think I'll need your help, Lisa. I don't want to do
it alone."

"You tell me when. I'll be there."

Maggie walked back to her room. Who would have
ever thought when she and Lisa were growing up that
they would be close now? They were still so different—oil and vinegar, Lisa said—yet they clung together, especially at times like this. Right now Maggie
needed Lisa like she needed the sound of the waves at
night, her tea in Jordan's sippy cup in the mornings,
and Kyle's constant friendship.

"I'm just going to jump in the shower," Maggie hollered. "Be out shortly."

"Take your time," Lisa called. "I'll just have another martini for the road. Hell, maybe two, since you're driving."

"I just have to jump in the shower," she continued. "Then I'm ready."

"Take your time," Lisa called. "I'll just take another minute in the tub. We have two more hours before Jarrett—"

EIGHT

Maggie's hands trembled as she stared at the mobile phone in her hand.

Her hands never shook. For heaven's sake, she was an emergency room physician. Every day people's lives rested in her unshakable hands.

"Want me to dial for you?" Lisa's tone, for once, was without edge.

Maggie glanced up. After all these years of selfishness, it was still hard to believe Lisa was here for her. That thought gave her courage. "No. I can do it."

They were parked on the street in front of an old brick warehouse near the waterfront in Philadelphia. The simple painted sign over the double glass doors read "McKay Industries."

Jarrett wasn't inside. Lisa had already gone into the building to check it out. Using her feminine wiles, she had discovered that this was Jarrett McKay's place of business and that he was not in Philadelphia, but on vacation at one of the Delaware beaches. Apparently Lisa's short skirt had come in handy.

"Well, either do it or give me the damned phone and I'll do it."

Maggie held the phone out of her reach. "I said I can do this." Her pulse was racing at least double its usual rate.

Lisa gestured with a cigarette. "Well then, do it, already!"

"Don't light that thing in my car."

"I'm not. Make the call."

Maggie stared at the phone in her hand again. "All right, all right." She took a deep breath and exhaled. This time her hands did not tremble. As she punched in the phone number, she realized it had the same exchange as her own. The son of a bitch was vacationing on *her* beach with *her* daughter.

The phone rang in Maggie's ear. One ring. Two.

Maybe he wasn't home.

She didn't know what she'd say if she got Jarrett's answering machine. Hell, she didn't know what she was going to say if she got him. *Hi, this is Maggie Turner. You remember me. I'm the mother of the little girl you took from me.*

A third ring.

He wasn't home. Damn. Damn. Damn.

Thank God.

A fourth ring.

Maggie knew what would happen next. Her own answering machine was set the same way. After four rings, the message would play. She couldn't leave a message on the machine. This was a phone call that had to be made person to person. She'd call again later.

Maggie was just about to hit the "end call" button

on the phone when she heard someone pick up. Her stomach fell.

"Hello, McKay residence," a teenish feminine voice said.

Oh, God it was *her*.

"Hello?"

"H-hello," Maggie stammered. She was stunned. Overjoyed. This was her daughter, had to be—the daughter of her body and of her heart, a daughter just as Jordan had been her son.

"This is Taylor," the girl said, sounding peeved. "May I help you?"

Taylor. Her name was Taylor. A perfect girl's name. Strong, but feminine.

"Um . . . yes. Yes. May I speak with your—" Maggie's tongue twisted in her dry mouth. "Is Jarrett in?"

"Sorry, he's catching a wave."

Maggie was so awestruck by the mere thought of speaking with her own daughter for the first time that she could barely keep up her end of the exchange. "Pardon?"

"He's surfing. High tide and a storm's coming in. Great breaks on the waves as they curl. May I take a message?"

Taylor definitely sounded impatient now. But teens were impatient, weren't they? It wasn't really Maggie she was annoyed with.

"Will you ask him to give Maggie a call? I'll be in after nine." She gave her the phone number.

Taylor repeated it back. She had excellent phone manners. "OK. Got it. Maggie who?"

Maggie felt her heart flutter. Taylor didn't seem to

react to her name. Had Jarrett ever said her name? Sure he would have. But how much had they ever spoken about her? Did Taylor know something of the woman who had given her life? Had he told her some of the details, what little he knew, or had he glossed over her entire existence by neatly killing her off in childbirth?

"He'll know who it is," Maggie said, her voice sounding stronger than she felt. "Just ask him to call me. Thanks. Good-bye."

" 'Bye."

Maggie listened to the buzz of the disconnected phone in her ear. Her gaze drifted to Lisa's face. "It . . . it was my daughter . . . Taylor," Maggie said softly, tasting the name on her tongue.

"Is she still on there?"

Maggie knitted her brows, the phone still pressed to her ear. "No."

"Then give me the G.D. phone." Lisa snatched it from Maggie's hand and dropped it into her purse between the two seats. "Now tell me everything. The suspense is killing me."

Maggie gripped the steering wheel. She'd called Tucson and Baltimore to find her child was in Philly with Jarrett. She'd gone to Philly to discover they were in Delaware on her very own beach. Unbelievable.

"So what was she like? Was she one of those sulky teenagers, or was she a smart mouth?"

"Neither." Maggie still held the wheel. "She was pleasant. Polite. She sounds like"—her voice cracked—"me."

"Jesus H. Christ Almighty. I need a drink." Lisa lit up the cigarette she'd been flailing.

"I said not in my car."

Cursing under her breath, Lisa threw open the car door and stepped out onto the sidewalk.

Maggie sat in the driver's seat for a moment, still overwhelmed. Finally she willed her legs to move and got out of the Jag. "He—she's right there in Talbany Beach," she said, coming around the back of the car. "Right under my nose."

Lisa took a long drag on her cigarette. "Renting for the summer?"

"I would suppose." Maggie had so many questions. There was so much she wanted to know about her daughter. How had Jarrett gotten her? How had he even found out she was pregnant? Did Taylor know Maggie was alive? What had he told her about Maggie's putting her up for adoption?

"Or maybe he's at his folks' beach house," Maggie told her sister.

"I thought you said they sold that place."

"I said it was locked up last time I went by. A for sale sign on it. I don't know that they actually sold it."

"Well, ain't that just swell." Lisa ground her butt on the sidewalk with her Italian sandal and reached through the open window to retrieve another cigarette. "There he is living near you and he doesn't even know it."

Maggie suddenly slapped the roof of her car, startling Lisa. "Get in the car!" She ran around to the driver's side.

"I was going to have another cigarette." Lisa jerked open the car door. "I need another cig, sis."

"I have to get home." Maggie pulled the strap on her seat belt and latched it securely. "No more cigarettes. Get in the car." She started the engine. "Or walk back."

Lisa got into the passenger's side and slammed the door shut as Maggie slid into first gear and shot away from the curb.

"With this skirt I could have hitched a ride," Lisa remarked tartly, stretching her long, bronzed legs. "I take it you're expecting him to return your call tonight?"

Maggie gripped the leather steering wheel with every bit of strength and determination she possessed. "He'd better."

Maggie arrived home at 8:35 p.m. The answering machine had recorded five messages while she was out. One was from Kyle, one from a salesman trying to peddle credit cards, and three were from a very angry Jarrett McKay.

When the phone rang at exactly nine, she was prepared in body and spirit. She had the cordless phone in one hand, a cup of hot tea in the other. She had planned what she would say. She was going to stay calm and in control of this conversation.

The phone rang once. Twice. Three times.

Lisa glanced up from the fashion magazine on her lap. "So are you going to answer it or let him leave another message on your machine?" She lifted one bleached eyebrow.

Maggie pressed the "on" button on the phone. "Hello."

"I wondered how long it would take you to pop up," Jarrett said.

No "Hello, Maggie, how are you?" No "How have you been these last fifteen years?" Just anger.

Maggie was surprised by the trip in her heart at the first sound of his voice after all this time. She remembered it as if only yesterday he had held her close in the front seat of his red Mustang and whispered that he'd love her forever.

"I hoped you'd have the good sense to stay away," he continued, making no attempt to hide his bitterness. "I hoped. I prayed. But I guess I should have known better."

"Jarrett," she said, trying to keep her voice steady as her heart pounded, "we need to talk."

"Nothing to talk about."

She gripped the phone. "Jarrett, she's *my* daughter, too."

"You should have thought about that fifteen years ago."

His comment stung, but she refused to be baited. They weren't teenagers anymore. She was an adult now and this was her daughter. "Jarrett, I didn't even know you had her."

"And your point is?"

He wasn't making this easy for her—not that she'd expected him to. But his anger was intimidating. *He* was intimidating. He was Taylor's father. He had raised her from a newborn. He'd fed her, changed her diapers, bought her first bra. Jarrett was everything to Taylor and Maggie was nothing. No one.

Maggie dug in. "Jarrett, I think we should talk in person."

"I told you I don't want to talk to you. I don't want you to talk to Taylor. I don't want you near her."

Somewhere in the depths of the anger in his voice, Maggie heard fear. Did she blame him? If the roles were reversed, if someone was trying to take her little Jordan, she'd be petrified. Of course, that didn't make sense. He *had* been taken from her.

Maggie forced herself to focus on her conversation with Jarrett. "I just want to see you," she said carefully. "At least for now."

"Maybe I should call my lawyer."

"I've already called mine."

There was silence on the phone.

Maggie hated to use legal threats, but she wouldn't be brushed aside. This was too important, too vital to resurrecting her shattered life.

"When do you want to meet?"

"Now," Maggie heard herself say. "If that's all right. I'm only a few blocks from your parents' old place."

He paused. "Taylor's at a movie with a friend, but I have to pick them up at the theater in an hour."

"Give me five minutes," she said quickly. "Just five minutes of your time."

"Meet me at Boat Drinks off the boardwalk in fifteen minutes."

Before she could reply, he hung up.

Maggie carefully set down the phone.

"So?" Lisa said as if she hadn't heard the entire conversation from two feet away.

"He's going to meet me in fifteen minutes. A bar."

"Oh, my God!" Lisa leaped out of the chair. "Fifteen minutes?" She grabbed Maggie's hand and pulled her off the couch. "You're going to have to hurry."

"Hurry for what?" Maggie dragged her feet. "It's just down off the boardwalk. A five-minute drive, even with finding a place to park."

"You've got to hurry and change and get rid of that cheerleader ponytail."

Maggie glanced down at her khaki cord beach shorts and brushed her hand over her short ponytail. "What's wrong with the way I'm dressed?"

Lisa pushed Maggie into the master bath and reached for the rubber band that held back the offending ponytail. "What's wrong with it? You look like a teenage beach bum. I wouldn't return a lost puppy to a woman looking like you do right now."

Maggie lifted her gaze to the mirror to meet Lisa's. *Return a lost puppy.*

Her words hung in the cool, air-conditioned air.

Is that what this is about? Maggie asked herself. *I want my lost baby returned and anyone will do? How pathetic.*

But no. That wasn't it. Jordan was gone. She knew that. Nothing and no one could bring him back. She couldn't change the past. She couldn't bring him back to life or return her infant daughter to her arms. But maybe, just maybe, she could alter the future. Maybe she could hold Taylor in her arms now.

* * *

Maggie recognized Jarrett immediately, yet he looked so different than she expected that she stopped inside the doorway. She had expected a businessman/lawyer type: short-cropped blond hair, khaki walking shorts, a polo shirt, loafers—a man who shopped in stores like Kyle's.

Instead he was dressed in an old pair of corduroy beach shorts similar to the ones she'd just shed. He was wearing a faded T-shirt with the name of a surfing company emblazoned across the front. His sun-bleached hair was shaggy and sorely in need of good cut. He looked older than she'd expected, too. Had raising their daughter aged him so?

But he was still handsome, still the boy/man she had fallen in love with so many years ago.

Maggie felt foolish. Surely she didn't still harbor feelings for him after all this time—not after what he'd done to her.

She walked up to the booth where he waited. "Jarrett."

He didn't look up. "Maggie."

He didn't offer her a seat, either. He was nursing a beer.

She slid onto the bench across from him and set her keys on the narrow table between them. "Thanks for seeing me on such short notice."

He lifted his head, his blue eyes meeting hers—the same eyes she'd lost herself in years ago. "Let's just cut the friendly chitchat, shall we? What do you want?"

He had been angry on the phone, but now he was downright hostile.

"What do I want?" She tried to collect her disengaged thoughts, remember her rehearsed speech.

"Yes, what do you want? You called me. You obviously want something."

OK, so this was how it was going to be—no small talk, no sense of old friendship. He wasn't going to cut her a break.

She looked him straight in the eyes. "I want to see my daughter."

He slapped his hand on the table. "Absolutely not."

Instinctively she drew back at the loud smack. He was angry? So was she. "She's my daughter."

"You gave her up. You gave her away." He gripped the handle of his beer mug so tightly she thought he might break the glass.

"No, I didn't."

He glanced up at her again, his voice thick with sarcasm. "You didn't?"

"No. I didn't," she said firmly. "That baby was taken from me. The adoption was illegal. I never signed any adoption papers."

He gave a snort. "That's what they all say."

"Well, *they* all may say it," she countered, "but in this case it's true. Your adoption of my daughter was illegal. And should I be able to prove it—which I can—that would mean you took my child from me illegally. That would mean I have a right to file for custody myself."

He didn't breathe. "You wouldn't dare."

She held his gaze. She didn't want to take Taylor from her father; she really didn't. She only wanted a little piece of her. She just wanted to get to know her, to have her get to know her own mother. But Jarrett didn't have to know that—not yet, at least. If he wanted to play hardball, she could play hardball.

She reached for her keys, as if the discussion was over. "If you won't be reasonable, I don't have any other choice."

NINE

"Wait." Panic tightened Jarrett's chest.

Maggie couldn't really take Taylor from him, could
she? He wanted to believe she couldn't. Their daughter
had been with him for almost fifteen years. The thought
that her birth mother could step in now was ludicrous.

But he read the newspapers, watched news reports.
Children *had* been returned to birth parents, even birth
parents who were homeless or had drug addictions.
Nothing in today's legal system was considered ludicrous any longer. In a world where common sense no
longer prevailed, anything was possible.

"You wouldn't really try to take her away from me,
would you?" Jarrett met her gaze and saw a flash of
the Maggie he had known. He was certain that, at least
for an instant, she understood his fear. "I'm the only
parent she's ever known."

"And I want to rectify that." She withdrew her hand
from her keys and sat down again.

Jarrett heaved a silent sigh of relief. She hadn't said
she *wouldn't* sue for custody, but it sounded as if she
wanted to be reasonable. Maybe she was just threaten-

ing him because she felt he'd backed her into a corner. Hell, for Taylor, he'd do the same thing in a minute.

Jarrett took a sip of his beer and tried to collect his thoughts. Over the years he'd planned what he would do, what he would say, if Maggie ever showed up on his doorstep. But when he'd rehearsed, he hadn't taken into account the feelings that would accompany her arrival.

Seeing Maggie like this after all these years had brought a flood of emotions he didn't want to deal with right now—ever, if he could help it. He had expected to be angry with her. What he hadn't expected was the strange tightening in his chest that was something akin to want, need. He experienced a sense of loss he hadn't felt in a long time, a sense of longing.

No woman had ever touched his heart the way Maggie had, not in all these years. He tried to tell himself maybe it was like that for everyone; maybe there never was a love like the first. But just maybe she had been different. Maybe their love had been different. He didn't know. He never would.

"Tell me what you want," he said, not looking at her this time. She was still so damned beautiful in a wholesome, natural way. Older, certainly more mature looking, but maybe more beautiful than he remembered.

"I told you. I want to see Taylor. I want to get to know her and let her get to know me."

"Why?" He rested both hands on the table. He tasted his bitterness again. "Why now, after all these years?"

She took so long to answer that he glanced up at her and then wished he hadn't. Her face was taut, her eyes bright and wide. For a moment he thought she might start to cry. He didn't want to share whatever pain was reflected in her eyes—didn't want to know, didn't want to care.

She didn't cry.

"Why do I want to see her? Lots of reasons. The biggest, though"—she paused and swallowed—"is that I've gotten to a point in my life where I want to make changes. Things didn't go the way I'd thought they would." There was a catch in her voice. "I know I can't change the past with Taylor, but I'd like to think I can change the future."

He drained his glass. He knew he shouldn't speak to Maggie without first contacting his lawyer, but Jarrett was a simple man living a complicated life. He liked to keep things as easy as possible when he could.

"Maggie, this is going to be hard. Taylor . . ." He let his daughter's name hang in the air between them. A jukebox played in the background and the smell of cheeseburgers wafted from the swinging kitchen door near the bar.

"She what?"

"She doesn't know you're alive," he said, settling on the truth.

"Doesn't know I'm alive?"

He glanced at her over the rim of his empty beer mug, thinking maybe the truth wasn't always best. His father had always told him it wasn't necessary to say the first thing that came to his mind.

"What would you have done if you'd been in my shoes? Would you tell your child that her mother gave her up for adoption because she didn't want her, or would you tell her her mother died? Which would be easier for both of you—certainly less painful?"

Maggie sat back, crossing her arms over her chest.

He was right and she knew he was right. He recognized the look on her face.

"You told her I was dead? How'd you kill me off?" There was a tone of sarcasm in her voice. "Childbirth, I suppose."

"No." He stayed cool, trying his damnedest to be distant. "I didn't want her to blame herself. I told her you were killed in a car accident."

Maggie gave a little laugh, but it caught in her throat and came out something like a sob.

Jarrett didn't know what was going on with Maggie, but he knew there was more than she was saying. Coming here now after all this time wasn't just a case of making amends.

"She's going to be angry with me," he told her.

"She should be."

"At both of us. *Very* angry."

"Maybe you should have thought of that when you chose not to tell her the truth."

"I should have thought of that when she was three? When she was watching *Sesame Street* and learning to put her own shoes on?" He sat back on the bench and flicked a piece of wet napkin across the table. "Yeah, right." He leaned forward again. "Maggie, you don't understand what it's like raising a child. You do what you think is best at every moment, at every fork in the road, and it seems as if there's one about every five minutes. You know, no one sent a care manual home with her from the hospital. I did what I thought was right at the time."

"I do understand," she said quietly.

She was looking at her hands. He noticed she wore no wedding ring, but she wore no rings at all. That didn't mean she wasn't married. Her statement led him to believe she had children, but he wasn't sure. "You do?"

She smiled a smile he remembered, one that had once made him warm inside. "I think all parents wish they'd come home with a manual. A serious one, not just Dr. Spock and *What to Expect . . .*"

"You have children, too?"

He had told himself on the way over here he wouldn't ask Maggie any personal questions. He was determined not to ask her any of the things he wanted to know, any of the things he'd thought about over the years. But he couldn't help himself.

"I did." She fiddled with her keys. "A son, Jordan. He was killed a few weeks ago in an automobile accident."

"God, I'm sorry Maggie." Jarrett deflated, feeling like an ass. His respect for her swelled. If Taylor died, he would shrivel up and die, too. But not Maggie. She'd survived.

"His father?" he asked.

"My husband was killed, too."

Silence hung between them for a moment, and then she glanced up. He was thankful she spoke so he wouldn't have to. He didn't know what to say.

"Listen, I'm not telling you about that to make you feel sorry for me. My family's death doesn't really have anything to do with Taylor. I mean it does, but it doesn't. Before the accident I wanted to find her, too. I just . . . I guess I didn't have the courage."

Jarrett was torn emotionally. He wanted fiercely to hang on to Taylor, keep every bit of her for himself. He was angry with Maggie—no, furious with her—for abandoning Taylor at birth. For abandoning him. But somewhere deep inside he wondered if it would be better for Taylor if she knew Maggie, maybe just a little.

Jarrett ran his fingers through his hair, which was still sticky with salt water. He hadn't had time for a shower. "I'm not sure what the best way to handle this is. I'll have to contact my lawyer."

She nodded. "I understand. I was hoping, for now at least, I could just meet her." She glanced up. "You wouldn't even have to tell her who I am for now."

He wanted to say no. He wanted to walk out the door and call his lawyer. But something made him hesitate. Something in him made him consider the proposal. He had to do what was best for Taylor—not for him, not for Maggie.

"What, you just want to show up for dinner?"

She shrugged. "If you like. You could tell her I'm an old friend—which would be true. It doesn't have to be dinner, or your house. We could go to the boardwalk, play some games, eat some fries." She smiled a little. "Don't fifteen-year-old girls play skee ball and eat fries?"

"By the bucket."

She picked up her keys and slid out of the booth. "Well, I'd better let you get going. You don't want to leave Taylor waiting for you."

"When do you want to do this?"

"You tell me. I work the next three evenings, but then I'm off for two. Would Wednesday evening work for you?"

"I suppose."

"Next to the fry place on the avenue and boardwalk, say six?"

"We'll be there."

She started to walk away, and he called after her. He didn't know why he couldn't resist. "Hey, Maggie."

"Yes?" She turned around.

Her hair was shorter than it had been when they'd dated and there were tiny lines around her eyes, but she was the same Maggie who had kept him awake nights long after she was gone from his life.

"Where do you work—in case I need to contact you before then?"

"Talbany General."

He watched the door swing shut behind her. He didn't have to ask if she'd become a doctor. He already knew the answer, because he lived with a female who was every bit as determined as Maggie had been.

"So?"

Maggie looked up to see Lisa leaning against the hood of her Jag. She wasn't surprised to see her, though Lisa hadn't ridden over with Maggie.

Maggie hit the automatic key in her hand and heard the car door unlock.

"Where are you going to see her? Was he hostile?

How did he look? Old?" Lisa put out her cigarette and got into the passenger side.

Maggie gripped the steering wheel and stared through the windshield at the rear of the car in front of them. "He's going to let me see her," she said, her voice trembling. "Just see her for now. I told him he didn't have to tell her who I was yet."

Lisa gave a hoot, slapping the leather dashboard. "You go, girl! I knew you'd be too tough for him. He crumbled, didn't he? He couldn't stand it. He was intimidated by the fact that you're a doctor. I knew he would be."

"I didn't tell him I was a physician," Maggie said softly. She was still in a mild state of shock. She had gone to meet Jarrett to convince him to let her see her daughter. She had gotten what she wanted, but only now did she realize what it meant. She was finally going to see and talk with the child she had given birth to, but never seen. After all these years of fantasizing, she would finally meet her.

"Didn't tell him? Why the hell not?" Lisa didn't give her time to answer. "So when are you going to see her? Is she coming to your place? Can I meet her? I'm dying to meet her, but if you want some privacy at first, I'll understand." Lisa talked faster. "I mean, after all, she's your daughter. I'm only her aunt."

"Lisa, Lisa." Maggie gripped her sister's thin forearm. "Calm down. You're making me crazier than I already am."

"I'm sorry. I'm sorry." Lisa pressed both of her palms to her hollow cheeks. "I'm just so excited. Aren't you excited?"

Maggie still clutched the wheel. "Of . . . of course I'm excited."

Lisa stared at her in the shadows cast by the streetlights. "You look petrified."

Maggie thrust the key into the ignition and the engine turned over. "I'm that, too."

"I say we both need a drink." Lisa slipped her seat belt across her waist. "What say we stop at that little bar around the corner from your place?" She laughed. "We can always walk home from there if we need to."

Maggie flipped on the headlights and pulled out of parking space. "Oh no, no alcohol for me." She lifted one hand off the wheel, her fingers stiff from gripping it so hard. "I've got to keep my wits about me. A hangover is the last thing I need right now." Her pulse still raced. "I have no clue what I'm going to say to her when I do meet her." She pulled off the avenue and onto the highway and glanced sideways. "Lisa, how did you get here, anyway?"

"My car. I just couldn't wait for you to get back to tell me what happened."

"Don't you want me to—"

"Nah." She fluttered one hand. "We'll get it tomorrow before you go to work. Now tell me everything, word for word, and don't leave anything out."

Jarrett knocked on Taylor's bedroom door.

"Enter, oh mighty one!"

Jarrett opened the door and stepped over a pair of jeans crumpled on the floor. He picked up the pants and two T-shirts, making his way to her four-poster bed. "So how was the movie?"

Taylor didn't look up from the book she was reading. She was stretched out on her back on her bed, pillows propped beneath her head. Her hair spilled across the pillowcase, almost the same spun red-gold color as her mother's.

"It was good. We had popcorn and licorice. Thanks for paying."

Jarrett's toe caught on a sneaker, and he pushed it under the bed with his bare foot. He picked up two glasses from her nightstand, one empty, the other filled with flat soda.

For the last hour he'd been trying to think of the best way to broach the subject of Maggie. He had decided to go with Maggie's idea of not telling his daughter who she was, at least for the time being—not until he spoke with his lawyer, who was away on vacation in the Bahamas. But for now, what harm was there in Taylor's meeting her mother? The truth was bound to come out now, anyway.

"Say, guess what?" He tried to sound casual despite the pounding in his chest. He was scared—scared of losing even one tiny part of Taylor, scared of the old emotions Maggie was dredging up.

"What?" Still she didn't look up from the book.

"That phone call was from an old high school friend of mine. Name's Maggie Turner. She's a doctor at Talbany General."

"That right?" She peered over the edge of the hard-bound book for the first time. "Hey, Dad, did you know a father used to be able to marry off his daughter as soon as she was born? That way he could make money off her from the get-go."

"I suppose I knew that." Jarrett held on to the dirty clothes and glasses for comfort. "That friend I was telling you about, she wants to meet you. I thought we'd meet her up on the boardwalk some night."

"OK, Dad. Whatever." Again she was lost in the pages of her book. "Hey, Dad, when you go out, would you shut off the overhead light?"

Jarrett had to smile. "Sure, sweetie." He leaned over and kissed the top of her head. " 'Night."

" 'Night. Love you."

"Love you more," he answered, as he always did. It was a game they had played for years. When he was really lucky, she said, "I love you a bushel and a peck and a hug around the neck."

Jarrett flicked the light off, leaving his teenage daughter bathed in the glow of her reading lamp. She looked so relaxed, so content, that he felt guilty. How was she going to react to the news that her mother was alive and wanted to be a part of her life?

He closed the door behind him.

Knowing his daughter, he had a feeling she would be pissed.

TEN

Maggie dropped coins into the parking meter and hurried toward the boardwalk. Vacationers thronged the avenue, taking their sweet time as they moved down the sidewalk hand and hand, pushing baby strollers, or eating ice cream cones. Lisa had wanted to come to lend moral support, but Maggie had made her stay home. Having Jarrett, Lisa, and Maggie's daughter all in one place at the same time was more than Maggie could deal with, especially when she considered Lisa's role in the fiasco that had brought them all to this point in the first place.

She slowed as she approached the end of the avenue that met with the boardwalk along the beach. Ahead she could see the designated meeting place: the fry joint.

Her palms were sweaty and her stomach was twisting. She wanted to see her daughter, of course, but at the same time she was afraid to. What if Taylor didn't like her? Worse, what if she didn't like Taylor? Even worse, what if they got along famously and Jarrett refused to let Maggie see Taylor again? Would Maggie be forced to go to court to seek joint custody? Was she strong enough to go through that? Could she put Taylor and Jarrett through that?

And what about Jarrett? Maggie hadn't seen him again after he left for Spain to be an exchange student. She had broken up with him the night he confessed he'd had sex with Lisa, and she'd never spoken to him again. Looking back now, she realized hers had been an immature reaction. Despite their age, maybe they could have worked things out, even with a baby on the way. But she'd been stubborn and childish and afraid. That, fueled by Ruth's ranting and raving, had been Maggie's undoing.

Stubborn was right. In all these years she hadn't spoken to Jarrett once, not until this week on the phone. She wondered if they needed to talk about the past at some point, come to some resolution. Or would it be better to just let the past lie? After all, nothing could be changed.

Somehow that seemed childish. How could they pretend none of it had happened when they had a daughter to prove it had?

Maggie halted in front of an ice cream shop and stared at herself in the reflection in the glass. She wiped at the trickle of sweat that ran down her temple, half tempted to turn and run. Was she crazy to want to see Taylor? What could she offer her? How could she convince Taylor to allow Maggie to be part of her life after all this time?

Maggie had to force herself to walk toward the boardwalk. She'd gotten this far. She wasn't going to chicken out now.

She spotted Jarrett immediately. He was seated on a

wooden bench along the beach, facing the ocean, watching the seagulls fly overhead.

"Jarrett," she called, lifting one hand in a little wave.

Unsmiling, he glanced over his shoulder. She couldn't see his eyes for the wraparound green sunglasses he wore, but she knew he wasn't pleased to see her. She couldn't help remembering how, in the past, he'd always greeted her with a smile.

"Maggie."

She wove her way through the crowd and across the wide boardwalk to sit beside him. There was no teenage girl to be seen. "Is she here?"

"She's here. I told you I'd bring her."

Maggie folded her hands nervously in her lap. She had changed clothes several times, settling on denim shorts and a T-shirt. "What did you tell her?" She surveyed the people seated on benches on both sides of them. He'd said Taylor was here. Where was she?

"Just that you were an old friend." His voice was terse.

"So where is she?" Maggie whispered.

He hesitated, then pointed down to the beach some ten feet below the boardwalk.

What Maggie saw took her breath away. Sweet God! It was the girl on the beach, the one she and Kyle had seen making sandcastles not long after Jordan was killed. An omen. A good omen. It just had to be.

Suddenly dizzy, Maggie exhaled slowly. Taylor was beautiful. Thin, but not overly so, with long blondish-red hair, a little lighter than Maggie's.

She was on her knees, sideways to Maggie, filling a

bucket with sand to add a corner tower to a castle she was building.

"Oh," Maggie breathed. "Jarrett, she's beautiful."

A smile crossed his taut face. She could tell he was trying to remain cool and distant, but he couldn't help himself. "She is, isn't she? As beautiful as—" He cut himself off.

Maggie didn't dare wonder what he had intended to say. She was too enthralled by the sight of the long-legged teen engrossed in her sand architecture.

Taylor turned her head, and the last rays of the day's sun shone on her suntanned face. She was without the thick makeup most fourteen and fifteen year olds on the boardwalk wore, her skin smooth and fresh. Her eyes were blue. She had a turned-up nose and a sprinkling of freckles across the bridge of her nose and cheeks.

Maggie ran a finger across her nose. Not her nose, but her freckles. Her hair. Jarrett's eyes.

She looked nothing like sweet Jordan.

"Want me to call her?"

Maggie couldn't take her tear-filled eyes from her daughter. "No." She laid her hand on Jarrett's on the bench between them, surprised by the familiarity she felt. "Not yet. Let me look at her another minute."

He slipped his hand awkwardly from under hers.

"I could sit here and watch her all night," Maggie said after several minutes ticked by.

"Yeah, well, that would be fine," he said tightly, "except that I promised her pizza and fries." He stood. "Taylor!"

She immediately looked up at her father and smiled

a smile that made Maggie's heart flutter. She was a happy child. Maggie could tell by the sparkle in Taylor's eyes and the sincerity of her grin. And she loved her father dearly.

"Let's go, Taylor. My friend Maggie's here."

"Coming, Dad."

Maggie watched as Taylor returned the sand bucket to a little boy, demonstrating its use first. She stood and brushed the sand from her shorts and then her hands and came up the steps to the boardwalk.

Maggie didn't have time to rehearse what she was going to say. Almost fifteen years just wasn't enough. Suddenly Taylor was there in front of her.

"Hi, I'm Taylor." She took the initiative and offered her hand. She shook Maggie's in a confident manner that Maggie had never possessed at fourteen. Jarrett had done an excellent job of raising their daughter. She could already see that.

"I think we spoke on the phone," Maggie managed, savoring the feel of her daughter's sandy hand in hers. Her daughter! Her daughter at last. Her chest tightened until she felt as if her heart had swelled until it rose and caught in her throat.

"Well, it's nice to meet you."

Reluctantly, Maggie released Taylor. "Nice to meet you."

"So." Jarrett clapped his hands. "Food first, or the arcade and then pizza and fries?"

"Whatever you want, Dad." She hooked her thumbs into her shorts. She was dressed similarly to Maggie, in denim shorts and a T-shirt, hers with a women's athletic company name emblazoned across the front of her small breasts. "I'm not too hungry yet."

Maggie watched the exchange between father and daughter, trying to keep her focus on Taylor. After all this time, seeing Jarrett like this was hard. Here was a man who had betrayed her, stolen her child from her, and yet, in only a few minutes, she could see that he was just the kind of man she'd been looking for when she settled for Stanley.

"The arcade it is, then." Jarrett motioned south down the boardwalk, avoiding eye contact with Maggie behind his sunglasses. "Ladies."

Maggie naturally fell into step between them. Her heart was still racing. Taylor was so damned sure of herself, so bright and articulate, and her eyes sparkled the way Maggie had remembered Jarrett's sparkling, as if he had some secret he was about to spring.

As they walked along the boardwalk making small talk about the smells of funnel cakes and caramel corn, Maggie's gaze strayed to Jarrett. Despite his terseness with her, he was everything Maggie remembered—still handsome, though in a more mature, adult way; smart; engaging; so loving with their daughter.

Seeing him like this with their daughter was more poignant than Maggie had ever imagined. Memories crashed through her head, overwhelming her—the smell of him, the sound of his laughter that was still just the same. She had loved him so much. She just hadn't remembered until now.

How could she have forgotten the burning love she had felt for him? She had never felt that love for Stanley or any of the men she had dated through college and med school. What was she supposed to do with all of the memories and feelings now?

"I'm not sure you want to challenge Taylor to a game of air hockey," Jarrett said. Father and daughter grinned at each other. "She plays a mean game."

"Learned from the best, didn't I, Dad?"

Maggie remembered playing air hockey with Jarrett on this very boardwalk, in the very same arcade they were walking into. Some things never changed.

"I'll get some quarters," he said, walking away.

"No, wait." Maggie started to dig into her shorts for the bills she'd stuffed in them, but he waved her back. "You stay with Taylor and get in line to play air hockey."

He disappeared into the swarm of sunburned beachgoers, leaving Maggie alone with her daughter for the first time in her life.

"You . . . you come here a lot with your dad?"

Taylor chose one of the two hockey tables and leaned against a cinderblock wall to wait her turn. Two boys in baggy surf shorts and T-shirts popped coins into the game table and watched Taylor admiringly from the corners of their eyes.

"All the time. I know it's touristy, but—" The teen shrugged.

Maggie nodded, feeling foolish. She didn't know what to say next to keep the conversation going, but she wanted to desperately. She wanted to know what Taylor was thinking, what she thought about everything, anything. She wanted to make up for all these lost years right here and now.

Taylor seemed to have her father's gift for casual conversation. "Dad says you're a doctor."

"That's right." She took her time in answering. She had never imagined she'd be so nervous with her own flesh and blood. "At the emergency room at Talbany General."

"Cool. Dad said he thought about doing that once." She wrinkled her freckled nose. "But he didn't think he had the drive to stick with it."

Maggie had promised herself she wouldn't ask Taylor about her father. Jarrett McKay's life was of no consequence to Maggie now. But she couldn't resist. For some reason she wanted to know about him almost as much as she wanted to know about Taylor. "I think he would have made a good physician. But then, he would be good at anything he did, wouldn't he?" She leaned against the wall beside Taylor, feeling a little calmer. "It's been a long time since I saw your dad. Just what does his company do?"

Taylor watched the air hockey game. "They write the instructions in English for all kinds of foreign-made kits. Mostly on how to put furniture together." She laughed. "We've got these pieces of rickety furniture all over the house that Dad has tried to put together using his firm's directions. You ought to come by and see the place. It's a hoot."

"I'd like that. I've never heard of such a business."

"Dad thought of it on his own. He didn't go to law school like Nana and Pop wanted him to. He went to business school instead, nights, so he could be with me in the daytime when I was a baby. He started the business in our apartment. He had his picture on *Business Man* magazine cover last month and everything."

Maggie made a mental note to go to the library and try to find that back copy as soon as possible. Against all logic, she was fascinated by every element of Jarrett's past and present. She told herself she needed to know these things for Taylor's sake, but the lie was a thin one. Lies to herself always were.

"Here we go, ladies." Jarrett appeared, jingling a handful of quarters.

"Just in time, Dad."

The two boys in surf shorts walked away from the table and Taylor stepped up, popping coins into the slot. "Ready to be slaughtered, Maggie?"

"Oh, no. I haven't played in years. Your dad—"

"Go ahead, Maggie. Play her." Jarrett gave Maggie an easy push in the small of her back.

His touch took her by surprise. In a flash, she remembered what his hands had felt like on her naked body, on her breasts, her thighs . . .

Maggie stepped in front of the table, shocked by her mind's betrayal. How could she be here meeting her daughter for the very first time and think about old sexual escapades?

"Ready?" Taylor asked, grinning across the table.

Maggie swallowed. "Ready."

Maggie played Taylor three games of air hockey and lost all three. By the time they'd played four games of skee ball, squirted water into castle doors, whacked rodents, and eaten two pieces of pizza each, Maggie was beginning to feel as if she and her daughter were old friends.

As the sun set at their back, Maggie and Jarrett took a seat on a bench at the far end of the boardwalk away from the crowds while Taylor wandered down onto the beach to scavenge for sand dollars.

"Thank you," Maggie whispered, watching the way the wind blew Taylor's silky hair across her shoulders. "Thank you so much for letting me see her. She's more than I—" A lump rose in her throat and she left her sentence incomplete.

It was so hard to express what she was feeling, even to herself, and yet she wanted to tell Jarrett. She wanted him to know how sincere she was in wanting to be a part of Taylor's life now. But the thought that such a life would naturally include Jarrett made expressing herself all the more difficult.

Jarrett sat on the bench beside her, his arm resting on the back, just brushing her shoulder. "How could she not be great? She's our daughter."

His words hung in the air for a minute, silencing them both.

"I wish I could tell you how sorry I am for the way things turned out," Maggie said when she found her voice. Just saying the words brought the ache back to her heart. "I never meant to hurt either of you."

He lifted one hand. "Let's not talk about this. I swore to myself before I came that we wouldn't get into this. Just the problem at hand. Nothing else."

"All right." She nodded, dabbing at the moisture in her eyes. She took a moment to collect her thoughts and get her emotions under control." The problem is that I want to see Taylor. I want to tell her I'm her mother."

He jumped up and struck the bench with his fist.

Maggie turned toward him, startled. Hurt, and she didn't know why.

He whipped off his sunglasses to gaze intensely at her. "Why don't you just say you want to screw up her life?"

Maggie covered her pain with anger. "Hers? Or yours?" The moment the words flew from her mouth, she regretted them. He had given no indication he was concerned with his own welfare. Since she'd first spoken to him, he'd thought only of their daughter. "Jarrett, I—"

"You always could get the best of me in an argument, Maggie." He crossed his arms over his chest, shaking his head. "You were always so quick. You knew how to hurt me." He took a deep breath, tucking his glasses into his shorts pocket. "I'm not worried about myself, and I say that sincerely. It's Taylor. This is all about Taylor."

She glanced down at her feet. "I apologize. I shouldn't have said that. I know it's not true. You want what's best for Taylor. It's what we both want."

A silence drifted between them. When Jarrett spoke, it was obvious he was trying to make peace. "So how's your mom and dad?" he asked.

He didn't ask about Lisa. Did he still feel guilty after all these years?

When Maggie thought of Lisa with Jarrett, the pain was just as sharp as it had been the night she found out—the night she had come home and confronted Lisa. Her sister hadn't even tried to deny it had happened, and she hadn't said she was sorry. As an adult, Maggie had come to understand why Lisa had done it. Lisa was so jealous of Maggie that the bad girl had needed to strike out at the good girl. Though the two women had never again discussed the incident, Maggie had forgiven her sister years ago. Could she forgive Jarrett now?

"My, um, parents?" Maggie stammered. It was so hard to carry on such a meaningless conversation when she was so wrought with emotion. "They're the same. Your parents?"

When she glanced at him, she realized by the way the corners of his mouth were pulled taut that he, too, was struggling.

He sat down on the edge of the wooden bench again. "They spend most of their time in Fort Lauderdale. They bought a house on a golf course. Dad plays; Mom gossips on the pool deck. Just what they always wanted." Again there was silence.

Maggie gazed out over the dunes at the waves washing in. She watched her daughter walk along the wet sand, tossing shells back into the sea.

Jarrett was waiting for her to say something, to somehow bring the evening to a close. She could feel it.

"So how do you want to proceed?" Maggie asked when she got her nerve. "I'd like to see Taylor again as soon as possible."

He leaned over, pressing his hands to his cheeks for a moment. "I suppose it was naive of me to think you'd be content just to see her, just to meet her." His gaze met hers. "You want more, don't you?"

Maggie sensed his fear. She could smell it on the

tangy breeze. He was afraid of her, afraid of how his life and Taylor's would be changed forever by Maggie's appearance after all these years.

A part of her wanted to reach out and pat his hand, tell him she would never take his daughter from him after what she'd seen between them tonight. But she couldn't bring herself to say the words—not yet, at least.

"Can I see her again this week," she asked, "or do you want to talk to your lawyer first?"

"He's on vacation."

"She and I could do something together. Alone. We don't have to tell her yet." Maggie's heart fluttered. She wanted to tell Taylor who she was here and now. She wanted to run down onto the beach and shout the words. She wanted to wrap her arms around her daughter and never let go.

But logic prevailed. It had to, because sound reasoning was the glue that held Maggie together. "Not unless you want to," she heard herself say.

He stood and stuffed his hands into his wrinkled surfer shorts. Maggie had never imagined this image of Jarrett, never fathomed this was what he would become; a beach bum of sorts with a multimillion-dollar business. Seeing him like this made her proud, almost as if she had somehow had something to do with the person he was today. Jarrett had broken from the mold his parents had made for him and had become his own man with his own interests and pleasures, his own business.

He groaned. "Let's put off telling her."

She felt a slight disappointment, though his words

were certainly not unexpected. "But I can see her again?" she asked hopefully.

Again he groaned. "Maggie, I don't know you." He searched for the right words. "How do I know you're not going to take off for God knows where with her?" He flung one arm toward the sea.

Maggie rose from the bench to stand in front of him. "You do know me," she said softly, feeling hot tears well in her eyes again. "Look at me."

Slowly, almost as if it pained him, Jarrett lifted his gaze from his deck shoes to her tear-filled eyes.

"You know me because I'm the same person I was when you loved me," she said, meaning every word. "I would never take our daughter. I would never jeopardize the relationship I hope—I pray—I can have with her."

His own eyes filled with tears as he held her gaze. "You wouldn't, would you?"

She shook her head.

"My lawyer is going to give me hell for this," he muttered.

She smiled hesitantly. She'd won! He was going to let her see Taylor again! "I'll just come to your place if you want. Hang out on the beach. You can keep an eye on us. We'll never even get in my car."

He stalled, thinking, considering.

Please let him trust me, she thought.

"Actually, I have to go to Philadelphia Monday, and I hadn't figured out what I was going to do with her."

"I can come over Monday! She'll be fine. She really will." She didn't want to beg, but she would if she had to.

"I'll be gone all day. Usually she goes to a girl-friend's or rides up with me, but—"

"Please, Jarrett, trust me. I've got a good job here that I love, friends. I'm not taking off for the border." She dared a little laugh.

He glanced sideways at her. "You don't have to work or anything? I mean, your being a doctor and all, you can't just take off when you want to."

"I work in the ER, but I can switch with a friend. It's not a problem."

A strange energy arced between them. They were still standing beside each other, close enough to touch if they had wanted to. There was something about standing side by side in the twilight, watching their daughter, that wove some magical thread between them that Maggie couldn't explain.

Jarrett could feel it, too. She knew it. She could tell by the way his breath had caught in his throat, the way his gaze lingered over her.

He glanced at his watch. "Well, um, guess we'll go on home. There's a movie she wants to see on TV at nine and I've got some paperwork to take care of."

"Taylor told me about your business, about how successful you are. Congratulations."

He glanced at her again, his eyes filled with pleasant surprise. "She did? Thanks." He looked away again, as if a little embarrassed.

"She's very proud of you," she said, proud of him, too.

"Not half as proud as I am of her."

Maggie watched Taylor walk along the white surf for a minute, and then she brushed Jarrett's arm. Again, his warmth brought back memories of the past—just flickers this time, but all the more unsettling. "I think I'll walk down and say good-bye. Thanks again. I can imagine how hard this was for you."

He stuffed his hands into his pockets again, staring out over the darkening horizon. "I only want what's best for her. We both need to focus on that and not ourselves."

Not ourselves. Jarrett's words echoed in Maggie's head as she walked down the timber steps and across the beach. *Not ourselves.*

Did that mean Jarrett was thinking about Maggie, too?

ELEVEN

Maggie arrived home to find Lisa gone. She'd left a note on the kitchen counter:

Decided to head home. Call you late. Hope it went well. Can't wait to meet my niece!

Love,
Sis

Maggie dropped the note on the counter. She wasn't surprised by Lisa's quick exit. The two sisters had been walking a tightrope since the whole thing with Taylor had begun by carefully ignoring the reason why Maggie broke up with Jarrett to begin with. Maybe her sister had a conscience after all. Maybe the pressure had been too much.

Maggie went to the phone, because Kyle would be waiting for her call. He picked up on the first ring. "Maggie?"

"Kyle." She didn't wait for him to question her. "You're not going to believe this. She was the girl on the beach, the one making sandcastles! She's so beautiful and so smart and not mouthy like so many teenagers I see in the ER. It was just incredible." Maggie was nearly out of breath, but she couldn't take the time to inhale. She had so much to tell Kyle, so much to hash over in her own mind. "We went to the arcade and played air hockey and ate pizza, and . . . and we just talked. Not about anything in particular, we just talked. We hit it off right away."

"And Jarrett?"

Maggie finally managed one deep breath. "What about him? He was fine," she said, a little too quickly. "He was good about the whole situation."

"So you hit off with him, too?" He sounded doubtful.

Maggie sank into the couch in the living room. "Well, no. Yes. I mean, not really."

"So you didn't get along?"

"Well, we didn't argue. I wouldn't do that in front of Taylor. We were supposed to be friends getting together. We didn't really talk too much. He's angry, of course."

"You can't blame him."

"Can't blame him? Him? What about me?" She kicked off her sandals and tucked her bare feet beneath her. *"He* ended up with my daughter—"

"His daughter, too," he interjected.

Maggie ignored him. "Without my knowing. What right does he have to be angry with *me?"*

"From his point of view, he did what was right after you abandoned the child he didn't even know—"

"I did not—" She cut herself off and let him continue.

"From his point of view, he's been the stand-up guy

here, and now he's getting put through the wringer. A single man takes the baby his ex-girlfriend gave up for adoption, raises her on his own until she's a teenager, and suddenly her mother appears and wants her back."

"I didn't say I was going to try and take her back."

"You told me you insinuated."

"Only because he was being an unreasonable ass."

"So that's why you're upset? Because he's an unreasonable ass?"

She moved the phone to the other ear. "I'm not upset. I'm excited."

There was a pause on the other end of the phone. Obviously Kyle didn't believe her.

"OK," she conceded. "I'm a little upset, but I'm excited, too."

"It's OK for you to be both at the same time, you know."

"What? Are you my psychiatrist now?"

He chuckled. "That is why we're here for each other, isn't it? Cheaper than a psychiatrist."

She lay back and propped her feet up on the back of the couch. This was Kyle she was talking to. She might as well spill her guts now and get it over with.

"I didn't expect to feel this way about him," she confessed. Surprisingly, her eyes grew scratchy and began to water.

"What do you mean?"

She wiped at her eyes with the back of her hand. "Hell, Kyle, I just buried my husband and baby. I shouldn't be—"

"Attracted to another man?"

"I didn't say I was attracted to him."

"Are you?"

"No. Of course not."

"No, you're not attracted to him?"

She closed her eyes with a groan. "No, I don't want to be attracted to him. That's sick. I just became a widow, for God's sake."

"But you and Stanley were over a long time ago, maybe before you ever got started. You once told me yourself you never got over Jarrett McKay."

Maggie rose and walked to the glass doors that lined the wall. She slid one open and stepped out onto the deck. The salty breeze caught her full in the face, clearing her thoughts.

"Maggie, you still there?"

"Yeah."

"So?"

"So this is stupid. I shouldn't feel like this about him after all this time. We were kids, for heaven's sake."

"Kids can be in love."

"He got me pregnant, had sex with my sister, and then went off to Spain, leaving me knocked up with no one to talk to but Attila the Mom. That's not the kind of man a woman is attracted to."

"Let's look at the facts. He *did* get you pregnant, or at least as much as you got yourself pregnant. He *was* drunk and didn't know it was your sister. He apologized and you broke up with him anyway. You never told him you were pregnant and—"

"Yeah, yeah, yeah," she said, growing angry. "The fact of the matter is he has my daughter."

"And you think you can have her back."

The cold reality of Kyle's words stung and her throat tightened. "I can't have her back, can I?" she asked in a small voice.

"If you mean can you take her from her father, erase his existence and everything he did for her, no. Afraid not, sweetheart. You're too smart to think that's possible, too good-hearted to try. But if you mean can you have a relationship with her now and be a mother of some sort, maybe."

She walked back into the dark living room and flipped on a light. "Do you always have to be so damned honest?"

"It's what you pay me for. Now back to the Jarrett topic."

"No, Kyle," she groaned. "Leave me alone."

"How does he feel about you? Is he attracted to you?"

"I feel as if we're in high school again."

"So he is attracted to you?"

"I don't know." She plopped down on the couch again.

"Do you care?"

"I don't know about that, either. This is just too complicated. I wouldn't want to fall into a relationship because it was easy. I made that mistake with Stanley. I won't settle again."

"Well, I say take it one day at a time, babe."

There was silence between them for a minute. "Thanks, Kyle. You're a dear. A great psychiatrist."

"Speaking of my aptitude, ding, your time is up. I've got a date."

"OK."

"Unless you'd rather I canceled. I could come over, bring a movie—"

"No, no, I'm all right. You go on your date."

"You sure?"

She smiled. "I think I've had enough of your honesty for tonight. Have a good time and call me tomorrow."

"Will do."

" 'Night," Maggie said.

" 'Night. And Maggie?"

"Yeah?"

"It's going to be all right. Things have a way of working out. Think positive."

"Think positive," she repeated. " 'Night."

Maggie hung up the phone and went to the refrigerator to get a diet soda.

Her meeting with Taylor had gone better than she would have guessed. But the whole interaction with Jarrett bothered her. She didn't care what Kyle said. How could those memories, those feelings, have come back so quickly, so easily?

So realistically?

She took a sip of the canned soda and the carbonation tickled her nose.

Surely she couldn't still be in love with him all these years, after what he did. Could she?

Maggie flipped on the stereo and walked in a circle around the couch. What had Taylor thought of her? Her gaze strayed to the phone lying on the couch. Instead of wondering, she should just pick up the phone and call Jarrett. She had a right to do that. After all, Taylor was her daughter.

But what if he didn't want to talk to her?

"This is ridiculous," she muttered, going to the couch. "I'm not in high school anymore."

She picked up the phone before she lost her nerve and punched in Jarrett's number, already memorized.

"Hello." His voice was all too familiar.

"Hi, it's me, Maggie." Now that she had him, she wasn't quite sure what she was going to say.

He sighed, not seeming surprised to hear her voice, but maybe a little reluctant to speak. "Yes, Maggie?"

"I . . . I was wondering how Taylor was."

"She's fine."

Maggie paced in front of the couch. "I know she's fine. I guess I was wondering what she thought about me."

"She thought you were one of my old friends." His tone was strained. "What do you mean what did she think of you?"

She ran her fingers through her hair in frustration. "Did she say anything about me? Later, I mean?"

"She saw you drive away. *Cool car* was her comment."

Maggie closed her eyes, leaning against the cool, dark glass of the balcony doors. "I really want her to like me, Jarrett. I think it will make it easier when we tell her."

He paused. She waited.

"Want to go for a walk, Maggie? Taylor's already cozied up with her movie. I'd rather talk in person than on the phone. I spend too much time on the phone with my business."

Maggie's heart gave a little leap. "Talk about Taylor? Sure. Now? You mean now?"

"I don't like to go too far from the house at night, but I walk on the beach a lot. Want to meet me halfway between our two places? I still can't believe you bought a house so close and I didn't know you were there."

Maggie was ecstatic—because they were going to talk about Taylor, of course, not about seeing Jarrett. "I'll start walking in your direction now."

"See you in a few."

Maggie grabbed a sweatshirt and ran out the back door.

Despite the hour, the beach was far from deserted. There were couples out taking romantic walks, as well as families getting a little exercise after a meal. Maggie met Jarrett almost exactly between their two houses.

"Mind if we walk back toward my place? Taylor's fine alone, but I like her to know she can find me if she needs me."

The cool breeze coming off the ocean raised goosebumps on Maggie's arms. She slipped her sweatshirt over her head. "Not at all. Where'd you tell Taylor you went?"

"Out for a walk with you."

They walked down to the waterline and headed north along the beach. "You told her?"

"Taylor and I try to be honest with each other. I don't have the time or the energy to be making stuff up and then trying to remember what I said—except for the big issue, I guess. About you."

Surprisingly, Maggie felt no anger this time. Maybe because deep in her heart, she knew that had the roles been reversed, she might have told Taylor Jarrett was dead, too. She nodded. "I guess that's the best way to raise a child."

"The only way."

They walked side by side, listening to the sound of the water lapping on the shore and the murmur of the wind. Maggie had so many questions about Taylor that she didn't know where to begin. She wanted to know everything—how old Taylor was when she took her first step, what her first words were, even when she had started her period. Yet something told her she and Jarrett needed to talk about themselves first before they could civilly discuss Taylor.

She took a deep breath and plunged in. "Jarrett, I'm sorry. It was wrong of me not to contact you and let you know I was pregnant."

He glanced at her, the moonlight reflecting off his blond hair, lending a golden magic to it. "We don't have to discuss this," he said tightly. "It happened a long time ago."

His suggestion was tempting. Talking about the past would be hard—hard for her, and apparently hard for Jarrett. But she couldn't push the past aside any longer. She'd been doing that for too many years.

"No, you're wrong. We do have to talk about it. I made bad decisions, decisions that have affected all of us. I was also eighteen years old, scared half to death, and alone, as far as I was concerned."

"It's not my place to judge you."

She halted to rest her hand on Jarrett's arm. "I should have written to you and told you, but my mother forbid me. She just took over. She sent me to live with my aunt in Tucson. She made all the adoption arrangements."

He crossed his arms over his chest. "I thought you said you didn't put her up for adoption," he said, his tone cool.

Maggie was suddenly close to tears. Her hand slipped from his arm. She started to walk again. "I didn't. I agreed with the adoption to begin with because my mother and my aunt had me convinced I had no choice, but I *did not* sign any adoption papers. I thought I would have time later—after—to make my final decision."

Maggie thought hard, trying to remember the night Taylor was born, but she could remember nothing of Taylor's birth but the blur of drug-induced sounds and the single cry of her daughter. And even those memories were mingled with memories of Jordan's birth to the point that she wasn't sure which memories were which.

After Taylor's single, lusty cry, Maggie remembered nothing until the following morning, when the baby was gone and she was being released from the hospital into Ruth's care.

She opened her eyes. "You know what my signature looks like. All you have to do is get a copy of my release. You'll know the truth then."

This time it was Jarrett who halted. He dug into the wet sand with the heel of his bare foot. "You're serious, aren't you?" His voice cracked with pain . . . fear, maybe.

She wiped her eyes with the sleeve of her sweatshirt. "Completely."

"Shit," he whispered.

"Yeah," she said.

He spread his arms wide, looking directly into her eyes. "So if you hadn't agreed to give her up, why did you wait all these years before looking for us—for her?"

"I didn't know she was with you. I thought she'd been adopted by some nice childless Tucson couple." She threw up her hands. "I was trying to do the responsible thing and let my daughter live the life given to her."

"Then your baby died," he said softly, his anger gone.

A flood of emotion filled Maggie. "Then my baby died."

Maggie smelled Jarrett even before she felt his arms around her.

"I'm sorry," he soothed, pulling her closely against him, wrapping his arm around her back. "I'm so damned sorry."

A sob rose up in her throat and she choked it back as her cheek came to rest on his chest. He smelled of suntan lotion, salt spray, and the love she had once known. His arms felt so good around her, good because she needed to be hugged, good because they were his arms.

She didn't say anything. She couldn't. She was too overwhelmed. And Jarrett said nothing. He just held her, smoothed her hair, and brushed his lips across the crown of her head.

"I never meant to hurt you or Taylor or anyone," she

said when she found her voice. "I didn't know you had her. I don't even know how you found out."

"It doesn't matter," he soothed. "I understand. We both did some foolish things back then, didn't we? And we were only kids."

Feeling in control again, Maggie took a step back. But the minute she moved out of Jarrett's arms, she wished she had the warmth and strength of them around her again. "Can't we work this out somehow?" she asked, hoping the desperation wasn't too audible in her voice. "Can't we?"

He turned to face the incoming tide and the great expense of the ocean and the horizon beyond it. "I think we have to, don't you? For Taylor's sake."

Maggie stared into the darkness of the ocean and a strange sense of peace came over her. "For Taylor's sake," she whispered.

"And mine," Jarrett said, taking them both by surprise.

TWELVE

Maggie laughed as Taylor relayed a story of a friend's attempts to dye her hair. After a long day of sunbathing on the beach, the two were chopping vegetables for salad in Jarrett's small kitchen. It had been Taylor's idea to surprise her father with supper when he arrived home from his business meeting in Philadelphia.

"Oh, no, not green," Maggie giggled, feeling more like a teen than she had in a decade.

"Like split pea soup." Taylor cackled. "No, no, worse! Like—like guacamole!"

Maggie dumped a handful of sliced cucumbers into a salad bowl filled with torn lettuce. "Well, I certainly hope you don't try that."

"Nah, I like my hair color most of the time." She scrutinized Maggie across the counter. "You know, my hair's almost the same color as yours, just lighter."

Maggie had to look away to keep from meeting her daughter's gaze. This would have been the perfect opportunity to tell her the truth, but Maggie wouldn't do that to Jarrett. They would decide together when to tell her, and how.

"Well, if we ever run across this girl on the board-walk, I want you to point her out. You never know when I might want a change. When you get to be my age, you start doing crazy things like dying your hair green and having the fat sucked from your thighs."

Still laughing, Taylor went to the sink to run water for the pasta. "Oh, you're not that old. You're the same age as my father—"

"Younger," Maggie corrected.

"And he's so young he still surfs and stuff."

Maggie nodded her approval. "Pretty cool dad."

"You ever surfed, Maggie?"

"Nope, but I'd be willing to try if you'd give me a lesson or two and promise to resuscitate me if necessary."

Taylor laughed again, her light, bright voice echoing off the ceiling tiles. The sound made Maggie's heart swell. Nothing could take away the pain of losing Jordan, but Taylor could certainly ease it.

"You know, when my dad said you and I were going to hang out together while he was gone, I wasn't thrilled with the idea. I mean, I know my dad doesn't like me to stay here alone when he's all the way up in Philadelphia. He's been, like, completely paranoid ever since he was on that magazine cover. They put things in the article about how much money he makes and about where I went to school and stuff. He was furious. Now he thinks someone's going to kidnap me or something." She rolled her eyes. "But I really am OK here by myself. Actually, it's kind of fun to be alone sometimes. Anyway, I'm glad you came over. I had a good time."

Tears sprang to Maggie eyes, and she brushed at them with the back of her hand. It was all she could do to keep from abandoning the salad to put her arms around her daughter. Instead she chopped onions. "I had a good time, too, sunburn and all. I spend so many hours at work that I don't get much time on the beach."

"Not even when you had your baby?"

Maggie's head snapped up in surprise. She hadn't known Taylor knew she'd lost her family.

Taylor's face fell. "I'm sorry. I shouldn't have said anything. I shouldn't have brought it up." She stared guiltily into the spaghetti pot.

"No, no, it's all right." Maggie returned her attention to the salad bowl. Her wound was still raw, but it wasn't bleeding. She could handle talking to her daughter about her son. "To answer your question, my son Jordan lived with his father in Washington, DC, most of the time. But when he was here, we loved to go down to the beach together. He and I used to spend hours making sandcastles."

The teen brightened. "I love making sandcastles. My dad's are the best."

"I know," Maggie said before thinking.

"You do?"

Maggie wasn't sure what to say now. She didn't know how much Jarrett had told Taylor about their past together. She decided a little information couldn't hurt. "Yeah, didn't you know your dad and I dated when I was in high school?"

"Sure. He told me."

"Well, we used to come down here to the beach when his folks had this place. He would build sand-castles for me on this very beach." She pointed with a paring knife.

"Cool. Sounds pretty romantic."

Maggie couldn't resist a smile, the kind two girl-friends would share. "It was."

"So what happened? Between you two, I mean." Taylor put the pot of water on the stove and turned it on. She turned to Maggie, wrinkling her freckled nose. "I'm sorry. There I go again. My dad says I'm too nosy."

"I think he's right," Maggie teased. "And you'll have to ask him about that one."

"Hey, was that my dad's car I heard?" Taylor walked around the counter into the living room. "You stay here and I'll run down. We'll surprise him."

Maggie watched Taylor run through the living room and out the back door. She leaned against the counter and took a bite of a carrot. Maybe making plans with Taylor to stay for dinner wasn't such a good idea. What if Jarrett didn't want her here?

But Maggie had shared a wonderful day with Taylor on the beach, so wonderful that she wasn't ready to see it end. What harm could there be in the three of them having dinner together? What reason would Jarrett have for not wanting her here? Hadn't he said he thought they could work this out somehow? Obviously they were going to be spending time together.

Maggie heard Taylor chattering as she bounded up the back steps. Behind her came the low rumble of Jarrett's voice.

"I hope you don't mind, Dad. Maggie and I are making your favorite, pasta."

From the doorway, Jarrett met Maggie's gaze. "Maggie."

The look on his face told her he did mind.

Maggie suddenly felt like an intruder and wished now she had gone home when Jarrett called on his cell phone to say he would be home in an hour. "Hi," she said. "Have a good trip?"

"It was all right." He handed Taylor his leather briefcase. He was not dressed as a business CEO in a suit and tie, but in khaki slacks and a short-sleeved black polo shirt. He looked slightly rumpled and utterly irresistible.

Maggie turned away from father and daughter, wondering if she should bow out of dinner gracefully. But she didn't want to hurt Taylor's feelings. "Salad's ready, Taylor. You'd better check the sauce on the back of the stove."

Just as Taylor ducked into the kitchen, the phone rang. "Can you get that, Dad?"

"I don't know why, it's never for me anyway," Jarrett picked up the phone, listened, then called to Taylor. "It's for you. Told you so." He held out the cordless phone.

Taylor ran out of the kitchen. "I'll get it in my room. Can you hang up when I pick up?"

"Certainly," Jarrett said with a mixture of amusement and sarcasm. "Anything else, darling?"

"Oh, Dad!"

Maggie heard Taylor's bedroom door close. A second later, Jarrett hung up the phone.

Maggie waited until she was sure Taylor was out of earshot. "I can leave if you want me to," she said. "Make up an excuse about the hospital needing me or something."

"No, no, that's all right. Taylor told me she invited you." He wandered to the counter that separated the kitchen and living room/dining room and took a seat on a barstool. "She has a right to invite you to dinner."

Maggie snatched up a wooden spoon to stir the boiling pasta. "Well, I certainly feel welcome now. Thanks."

"I didn't mean it that way. Don't go."

She turned from the stove to meet his gaze. "You're sure?"

"I'm sure. So how was your day on the beach?" He fished a slice of cucumber from the salad bowl.

She glanced at him across the marbled counter. This felt so weird, being here with Jarrett and Taylor, making dinner, asking how each other's day went. It was almost as if they were a family—but of course they weren't. "Good, really good. You've got a hell of a nice young lady there."

Jarrett reached for another cucumber. "You mean *we* have."

Maggie's gaze met Jarrett's. "We," she said softly, her smile hesitant.

Jarrett ran the fingers of one hand through his blond hair, leaving it standing up on end in an entirely too charming way. "So I guess we need to tell her about us—you—before things go too far."

Maggie watched his expression carefully. He didn't

seem angry at all tonight, just resigned, maybe still a little bit fearful. At least she had proved to him she could be trusted. She didn't grab Taylor and run the first time she had a chance. "I think you're right. It's time we told her."

Jarrett exhaled slowly. He acted as if he'd had a hard day and wasn't certain he was up to this tonight. "Do you think I should do it alone, or should we do it together?" He spoke softly so as not to risk being heard beyond the kitchen, his voice lending an air of intimacy.

Maggie studied the wooden spoon in her hand. "I suppose it's only fair to do it together. After all, I'm as much responsible for her not knowing the truth as you are. Maybe more. If I hadn't—"

"Maggie, don't." Again Jarrett sighed. "How did we get to this point?" His tone was wistful. "We had so much going for us. How could it all have gone so wrong?"

"Doesn't matter." She set down the knife and rounded the counter into the living room. He pushed a barstool toward her and she sat beside him. "What matters is what we do now. How we handle this now."

"You're right. I know you're right. I'm just dreading this. I hate having to come clean, especially with lies that are almost fifteen years old." He gave an ironic chuckle. "Boy, I could use a beer right now."

"Want one?"

"Nah, this is going to be hard enough as it is. I don't need to be in any form of an altered state."

Maggie nodded, putting her folded hands on the bar

beside his. "I know what you mean," she commiserated. "I'm not looking forward to it, either."

Taylor's bedroom door opened and they heard her coming down hall.

"Well," Jarrett said, covering Maggie's hands with one of his. "Let's get dinner on the table and get this over with, shall we?" He rose from his stool. "Then we can both have a beer," he whispered. "We ought to really need one by the time she goes to bed."

Maggie was so nervous as they put dinner on the table together that it was all she could do to engage in pleasant conversation. She wanted Taylor to know the truth, but now that it was time to tell her, she was getting cold feet.

She tried to tell herself it might be better if she went home and Jarrett told Taylor alone. But Maggie knew that was just copping out. It wouldn't be fair to Jarrett or to Taylor to make her father tell her.

Still, that didn't mean Maggie wasn't scared. She and Taylor had been getting along so well that she hated to have her daughter be angry with her now. But Jarrett was right. Taylor had to be told now, before the relationship went any further.

The three sat down to dinner, passing around bowls of pasta and sauce and salad. As they ate, they laughed and talked about nothing in particular. About halfway through the meal, when there was a lull in the conversation, Jarrett spoke.

"Hey, Taylor, Maggie and I have something we want to talk to you about. Something kind of serious."

Taylor looked up from her big plate of salad. "What?

You and Maggie have been dating secretly and you're in love, want to get married, and want my permission?"

Only Taylor laughed.

Maggie stared at her plate, wishing she could be anywhere but here at this moment.

"No, this is serious, sweetie." Jarrett took his time as he set down his fork, gathering his thoughts. Apparently he was the self-appointed spokesman, which was fine with Maggie. He knew their daughter better than she did. He would know what to say.

He wiped his mouth with a paper napkin from a fast-food place, all Maggie had found in the cupboard. "I'm just going to come out and say this because I can't think of any way to beat around the bush."

The teen stabbed at a piece of lettuce on her plate. "OK, already, Dad. I'm listening. What could be so terrible?"

"Taylor, I haven't been entirely honest with you about your mom."

Taylor put down her fork, eyeing her father suspiciously. "My mother? You want to talk about my mother now?" She glanced at Maggie, then back at her father. "Right now?"

He lifted his hand. "Hear me out. I did what I've always thought was right at the time. I've always told you that. But in the light of new . . . evidence, I've realized now that I was wrong, and I need to rectify the matter."

Maggie watched Taylor carefully. Her daughter was obviously confused. She had no idea where her father was headed.

"OK, Dad, out with it. You're scaring me."

Jarrett glanced at Maggie, and his face was so full of torment that Maggie feared this was all a big mistake. She didn't want to hurt Taylor or Jarrett; she just wanted to be a part of her daughter's life.

Jarrett must have sensed what Maggie was feeling because, to her amazement, he reached under the table and patted her bare knee.

His small gesture of kindness gave her the courage to speak up. "Taylor, what your father is trying to tell you is that your mother is alive." She looked directly into her daughter's eyes because she couldn't bear to look away. "And I'm your mother," she finished softly.

Taylor appeared stricken. She looked from Maggie to her father and back at Maggie again. "It's not true," she flared. "My mother is dead. She died in a car accident. I don't have a mother, just my father. Daddy?" The teen's eyes filled with tears as she looked to her father for affirmation.

Maggie placed one hand on the table in Taylor's direction. She didn't dare touch her, but she wanted desperately to reach out to her. "Don't worry, I'm not going to take you away from your father. I just want to—"

"Nothing between you and me will change, Taylor," Jarrett said firmly. "I love you and I will always—"

Taylor flew out of her chair. "How could you?" she shouted. Her gaze fell on Maggie and then darted back to her father accusingly. "I don't believe you!" She dashed at the tears filling her eyes. "I can't believe you would do this to me." She slammed the back of her chair and it struck the table. "I hate you! I hate you both!"

Taylor ran down the hall.

Maggie rose from her chair, tears brimming in her eyes.

"No," Jarrett said, laying one hand gently on her forearm. "Let her go. Let her be angry with us for a little while. She certainly deserves it. Let her get used to the idea, and then we'll go in and talk to her."

Maggie walked to the glass doors that ran the length of the house and looked out on the beach. She was feeling pretty shaky. "Boy, when you said she was going to be mad, you weren't kidding."

His chair scraped as he rose from the table. "She can be pretty emotional, but she's a sensible kid. Just give her a little time and she'll be all right."

Maggie fought her tears. "I hope this was the right thing to do," she said, not sounding too confident. "Maybe it would have been better if we hadn't said anything—if I hadn't shown up."

"I don't want to hear that." Jarrett came up behind her and put his arms around Maggie.

At first, his gestured startled her, but the feel of his embrace was so reassuring she couldn't help but relax.

"Every girl needs a mother," he said quietly into her ear.

They both stared out at the breakers, him looking over her shoulder. "And every girl deserves a mother like you."

His kind words struck her so hard that for a moment she thought she would burst into tears. But she didn't.

Instead, she just stood there, staring at the waves, enjoying the moment.

She tried not to think about this touching, this camaraderie between her and Jarrett, or where it was going. She could only deal with one crisis at a time.

THIRTEEN

Jarrett sat back in his plastic lawn chair on the deck outside his living room and propped his feet on the rail. He couldn't see the ocean in the dark, but seeing it wasn't necessary. He could hear its waves as they lapped on the shore, could smell it in the salty air, could feel the brackish spray carried on the night breeze. Out here on the balcony, surrounded by the ocean, he could sort things better in his mind.

He glanced at Maggie sitting beside him, sipping a cup of hot Lipton tea he had made for. He knew she preferred herbal teas, but it was all he had in the house. He made a mental note to pick up some herbal tea next time he was in the grocery store.

"So what now?" Maggie asked, her voice sounding distant.

Taylor's reaction had hurt her, he could tell. Even though he'd warned her Taylor would be very angry, she was still bruised by the teen's outburst.

"What now?" He leaned back in his chair. While Maggie's liquid consolation was a comforting cup of tea, his was a bottle of imported beer. He tipped the bottle and let the cold, refreshing ale run down his throat.

"Sure, what do we do? What do I do? Do I wait for Taylor to contact me? Do we make her see me whether she wants to or not? What do we do now that we've dropped this bomb into her lap? I hate to force her into anything she doesn't want to do, but she's not going to get to know me without seeing me."

"Right now I think the only way we could get her to see either of us would be to force her." He grinned at Maggie over the rim of the bottle. If there was one thing he'd learned raising a child, it was that you had to have a good sense of humor. An adage of his grandmother's often echoed in his head: *It's either laugh or cry, so you might as well laugh.*

She made a face at him. "Very funny."

Her expression made it clear that she didn't see any humor in the situation, but she was trying to follow his lead and stay upbeat. He knew one thing for sure about Maggie: She was a survivor. Only a survivor could have lived in the household she'd lived in, been forced to give up her baby, and still managed to grow into a responsible, emotionally healthy adult. Only a survivor could have endured the death of her husband and second child and still been able to smile, to make others smile. He admired her. He didn't know if he could have been as strong.

"I'm serious. I don't know what to do. Jordan was just a preschooler. I don't have any experience with teenagers."

Her face changed when she mentioned her son. He

saw the pain in the tiny lines around her mouth, heard the catch in her voice when she spoke his name.

Jarrett had never known Jordan, but it broke his heart to think about the little boy. Whether he wanted to admit it or not, it broke his heart because it broke Maggie's. And even after all these years, after her betrayal that cut so deeply he still bore the scars, he still cared about Maggie a great deal, and the idea was scaring the hell out of him.

He stared out over the rail. "As the father of a teen, let me tell you there is no such thing as experience with teenagers."

"Jarrett, you're not being particularly helpful here," she chastised, but not angrily. "Taylor's upset. I'm upset. You've got to be upset. I mean, it's not as if you were expecting me to walk into your life like this."

"You can say that again." He nodded and finished the beer. He had dreamed of it, but certainly never expected it. If she only knew how he'd longed for her in those first days with a crying, colicky infant and no one to keep him company but the hum of early morning TV.

She eyed him. "What's that supposed to mean?"

A part of him wanted to brush over his own comment and what it implied, but a part of him wanted to come clean. They were adults now, not teenagers. Hell, he could run a multimillion-dollar company. Surely he could tell a woman he had feelings for her.

He brushed her bare foot with his. "Come on, Maggie. You know exactly what I mean. Tell the truth. You didn't expect to be attracted to me after all these years."

Maggie looked too stunned to speak. Was she surprised he would admit he was attracted to her, or wasn't she in the least bit attracted to him? That thought hadn't occurred to him. He thought he'd felt caring in her touch, heard it in the tone of her voice whenever they spoke to or saw each other. But maybe he had gotten his wires crossed. If she wasn't attracted to him, he was making a complete ass of himself.

"I . . ." she stammered. "Well, I wouldn't say—"

"I'm not saying we have to do anything about it," he added quickly, still not sure if her reluctance was in admitting she still cared for him. "I'm not saying we would want to. I'm just saying it's a fact, and I wasn't expecting it." He frowned, feeling more foolish by the second. He was already knee-deep into this conversation; he figured he might as well go in with chest waders. "You *are* attracted to me aren't you, Maggie?"

She started to say something and then stopped. "Are you always this forward?"

"Truthfully? Yeah, I suppose I am. I'm pushing forty. I've got a company to run and a teenager who makes me crazy when I'm not loving her half to death." He wove his fingers together and cracked his knuckles. "I don't have time for nonsense." *And I don't have time to be hurt by you again,* he thought. "Not in my business life and certainly not in my personal life."

Jarrett waited; still she didn't speak. "Have I spoken out of line here?" he asked. "What I mean is, does your silence mean you *don't* feel this thing between us? Because if that's true, I'm going to feel mighty foolish here in a minute or two."

Maggie set down her mug and rose from the chair to lean on the salt-treated wooden rail and gaze out into the darkness. "Jarrett, my husband hasn't been dead very long."

She did care. He could hear it in the brittle tone of her voice. Against all reason, his heart gave a little kick. It had to be true what people said—a man never got over his first love. He knew he hadn't.

"I understand that. But, Maggie, feelings are not logical. They don't follow any rules of etiquette or social standards." He rose and stood beside her. On impulse, he covered her hand with his. Part of him was still so damned angry with her, but part him wanted her. Needed her. He needed her to fill the void she had left in his heart so many years ago. "I'm not saying we have to do anything about it; I'm just saying my feelings for you—my unexpected feelings—could complicate your relationship with Taylor."

Her hand was warm beneath his, stirring feelings and desires he thought he'd gotten over long ago. Jarrett didn't want to consider the possibility he and Maggie could reconcile. A loving relationship and a mother for his daughter? It was too big a dream, too sure a disaster in the making. She had broken his heart once. He wasn't certain he could bear to have his heart split in two again.

Jarrett felt Maggie's hand tighten beneath his as she gripped the rail harder. "Yes," she said softly.

He thought he knew what she meant, but he had to hear it from her own mouth. He couldn't rely on his own interpretations of her words and actions any longer. "Yes, what?"

"Yes, I'm attracted to you," she said in a small voice.

"I didn't expect it, and it scares the hell out of me, but . . . I am."

So she was as fearful as he was. Somehow he found that consoling. He patted her hand, his pat becoming a gentle caress. "Isn't that what being adults is all about? Being scared half to death most of the time?"

He brushed his fingers across the back of her hand, down her fingers. "I know that's the case when it comes to raising a daughter." He lifted his hand and rested it on her far shoulder.

"Well, I've been thinking about this even if you haven't," he continued, feeling her need for him to take control of the situation. "Let's not worry about you and me right now. Despite our physical attraction, I think deep down we're still pretty pissed with each other for reasons that can probably be justified. Let's just worry about Taylor right now and go from there. Does that work for you?"

Maggie was standing so close it would have taken little effort to lean over and kiss her lips—lips he still dreamed of.

What he had said was true. He was still angry with her, and he knew she was still angry with him. After all, he was the one who had betrayed their love by having sex with Lisa. But, damn it, he had been twenty years old. Just bringing these emotions out into the open and admitting them somehow dissipated much of the tension and anxiety.

"OK," she said shakily. "One thing at a time."

"First Taylor, then maybe you and me," he whispered. He was stepping into dangerous territory, but he couldn't help himself. He brushed a lock of her hair back, tucking it behind her ear. She smelled so good. She felt so right in his arms.

For a few minutes they just stood there, and he enjoyed the feeling of having her so close.

"Why don't you go on home now?" Jarrett said finally. "And I'll go in and see how Taylor is doing."

She made no attempt to remove his arm from her shoulder, so he stayed where he was.

"You don't want me to . . . I can go in and—"

"No," he said firmly. "I think it might be better this way. I'll call you in the morning and let you know how she's doing. Maybe we could go to a movie or something tomorrow night together, show her you're not going to go away even if she wants you to. I think that would be good for her. When do you work next?"

"Actually, I go on days starting tomorrow, so I'm free."

"Where's your beach bag and stuff?"

She seemed reluctant to step away from his embrace. "Already in the car."

"I'll walk you."

He followed her down the dark stairs and out to her car, which was parked beneath a streetlight. She acted as if she felt awkward as she clicked the keyless entry gadget, first locking it again with a beep, then unlocking it.

He had to smile. "Maggie?"

She turned to face him and he forgot what he wanted to say. All he knew was that he wanted to kiss her . . . had to kiss her.

Before she could pull back, he kissed her softly on

the mouth. " 'Night," he said, wanting a deeper kiss, but not daring.

" 'Night," she whispered and brushed his lips with her fingertips.

Then she hopped into her green Jag and was gone before he could think or speak, his mouth still tingling from her touch.

"A Coke and popcorn," Taylor said crossly. She stood beside her father, on the far side of Maggie at the concession stand of the theater, her arms crossed over her chest, her lip-glossed mouth stuck out in an exaggerated pout. This evening Maggie's articulate, mature daughter was the epitome of the sullen teen.

Jarrett glanced at Maggie, acting as if he had to bite his tongue to keep from laughing aloud at Taylor's antics.

On the ride over, both adults had tried talking to Taylor. They apologized again for their deception and explained why Jarrett had thought it best not to tell Taylor the truth. They tried to reassure her that having a mother could offer nothing but advantages, that her life with her father was in no way threatened by Maggie's presence.

Taylor tuned them out. She was angry and she was hurting and she wanted to punish them both.

Maggie tried not to be hurt too much by Taylor's behavior. Putting herself in her daughter's place, she could understand it. Taylor had to be both angry and afraid—angry with their deception, afraid of what the future would bring. Teens never liked the unexpected.

Maggie tried to echo Jarrett's easygoing attitude. He had more experience with their daughter; he knew how to handle her. Instead of continuing to discuss the issue, he had told Taylor they could table it until she was ready to talk. Now he was attempting to enjoy an evening out and he encouraged Taylor to do the same.

"Do I have to sit with you?" Taylor was dressed in tight shorts, a T-shirt that bared her midriff, and platform sandals. In choosing her attire, she had, no doubt, been trying to bait her father. Apparently he hadn't taken the bait, because Maggie hadn't heard a word pass between them about the bare tummy or the bright blue eyeshadow and sparkling lipgloss.

Taylor stared beyond Maggie and Jarrett at the heaps of popcorn behind the glass concession stand wall.

"You do have to sit in the same theater," Jarrett said. "But I don't suppose you have to sit right next to us."

Maggie had to smile. He was managing this situation better than she would have without his help. He was a good parent, his skills well honed. He wasn't making light of Taylor's pain, but he was trying to keep her from dwelling on it.

Jarrett placed an order for all three of them. "And M&Ms?" he asked Maggie. "You still like them?"

She was digging in her purse to find money. She couldn't believe he remembered. "Sure," she said with a smile. "Let me get this."

"Nah, you paid for the tickets. Let us get the snacks."

They paid for the popcorn, drinks, and candy and

went into the theater. Taylor took her popcorn and soda, without so much as a thanks, and went to the far side of the theater.

"So much for a movie together," Jarrett said. "These seats all right?"

"Fine." Maggie sat beside him and offered him the bag of popcorn. "She is going to be all right, isn't she? Do you think she needs to see a counselor or something to help her get through it?"

"I think she'll be fine. At breakfast she went on a five-minute tirade about how angry she was that I didn't tell her you were alive. Then she went for every detail. She wanted to know why you gave her up, why I took her, and what took you so long to find her."

"Did you tell her?" The popcorn tasted so good that Maggie took another handful.

"As much as I knew." He shrugged. "And from my point of view, of course. Eventually I think she'll need to hear the story from you, too." He glanced at her. "When you're both ready."

Just the thought of having to discuss the private adoption sent a tremor of fear through Maggie. But she could do it when the time came, for Taylor's sake and for her own.

"So how'd she take what you had to say?" Maggie asked quietly as the theater began to fill up.

"Actually, I think she understands. I told her to imagine what it would be like if she was pregnant now and felt there was no one she could turn to. I had to tell her a little about your mother."

"Oh, you don't know the half of it," Maggie said, remembering the ruse she'd been forced to employ of not letting him know where she lived or what her parents did for a living.

He tossed a kernel of popcorn into his mouth. "Actually, I know more than you think."

"Oh, God," Maggie groaned, sliding down in the seat.

"When I came back from Spain, I tried to find you, you know. I found Bob and Ruth."

She raised one hand. "Keep talking and I swear I'm going to shrivel up and die of embarrassment right here in this seat."

He laughed and patted her knee. "It's all right. We've all done some crazy things. Hell, I've met Ruth in her natural habitat. I can see why you lied to me. I'd rather have lived on Ivy Drive, too."

Maggie laughed with him, relief filling another aching part of her. She had hated hiding the truth of where she lived, who she really was. It had been difficult even as a teen to live a lie, especially with Jarrett. She had loved him so much. "So you got the gist of my double life?"

He nodded. "Must have been hard." He paused and then looked up to meet her gaze. "You could have told me, you know. It wouldn't have made a difference to me. I'd have felt the same way about you."

She smiled sadly. "I know you would have. I just didn't know it then."

He plucked at his T-shirt. "Do they know you found us?"

She shook her head, not trusting her voice.

"When are you going to tell her?"

Suddenly Maggie wished the movie would hurry and

begin. She wasn't ready to talk about Ruth, about the full extent of what her mother had done to her. She wasn't ready to think about resolving any of the issues, though she knew in her heart they had to be resolved before she could ever really be whole. "I . . . I've been thinking about going to see her. Telling her in person."

"You need to talk to her about it."

Maggie nodded, a lump in her throat. "I know."

He brushed his shoulder against hers. "I'd go with you if you wanted me to."

"You would?"

"Sure." He lifted a shoulder. "I could deflect the blows."

She eyed him. "Verbal or physical?"

He patted her knee. "Whatever you need."

The big screen flickered and the lights went down.

"Hey, share those M&Ms?" Jarrett asked.

Maggie offered him the bag and the hint of a smile. She almost felt as if they were on a date. He had even draped his arm casually over the back of her seat, maybe because there wasn't much room and that was the most logical place for him to put his arm. But maybe, just maybe, it was there because he wanted it to be.

"So did you sleep with him?" Kyle walked behind Maggie and placed an avocado in her shopping cart.

She looked at him as if he'd grown an extra head. "No, I haven't slept with him. How could you say such a thing? My husband hasn't been dead three months."

Kyle ducked as she tried to elbow him and added

shallots and fresh cilantro to the basket. "Just asking. Sounds like you're headed in that direction. I know these things."

"I'm not sleeping with him," she said a little louder than she'd intended to.

Maggie looked away in embarrassment as a middle-aged woman bagging Red Delicious apples stared at them. "Right now we're just trying to get Taylor used to the idea of having two parents. Jarrett and I haven't really discussed 'us' per se."

"So have you kissed?"

She must have looked guilty, because he didn't give her a chance to respond. "Aha! You *have* kissed," he accused with delight. "You kissed Jarrett McKay."

"Actually, he kissed me." She grabbed the cart and pushed.

"But you kissed him back, didn't you?"

"Do we have to talk about this in public?"

"Sounds like the relationship is going pretty well to me," he said in a singsong voice. "I hear more enthusiasm in your voice lately than I ever heard concerning good old Stanley. God rest his soul."

"Kyle—" She held up one hand. No matter who or what Stanley had been, she would not speak ill of him or listen to others do so.

"I'm sorry. You're right. I shouldn't besmirch a dead man's character. I'm just being honest."

"You're being honest. Jarrett's being honest." She surveyed the fresh vegetables. "What is it with the men in my life these days? What happened to those caveman stares and grunts? Life was a hell of a lot simpler when men weren't telling me their deepest, darkest feelings."

"Aren't we touchy today?"

She pointed. "Get bananas. You can make Bananas New Orleans. It used to be Jarrett's favorite dessert."

"Aha." Kyle waggled a finger. "See, what did I tell you? First you're playing footsie on the balcony, then movies and walks on the beach. Stolen kisses. Now his favorite dessert. This is all headed in the same direction—hot, sweaty sex."

"Kyle!"

He leaned to whisper in her ear. "Hot, sweaty, good sex. The kind that makes you scream."

She tried not to smile. "I don't scream."

"Not with Stanley, maybe." He lifted one eyebrow suggestively. "But with Jarrett, who knows?"

Just talking about sex with Jarrett warmed her to her toes. If she weren't only in her thirties, she would have sworn she was having hot flashes. She shoved the shopping cart forward. "Enough talk about Jarrett."

"All right." Kyle placed his hands on the cart beside hers, helping her push. "What about Taylor? She coming around?"

Maggie had to smile. Kyle was a good friend. He knew what questions to ask. He understood how important Taylor was to her. "She's still angry, but I think she'll come around. Jarrett does, too. For a while she wouldn't even acknowledge my presence. Now she at least says hello and good-bye. When I left the message on their machine asking them to dinner tonight, Taylor was the one who called me back."

Kyle added a fresh ball of Parmesan cheese to the cart. "Her father didn't make her?"

"Maybe, but that's OK. The point is she called and

actually talked to me. It may not be much," she admitted, "but it's a start."

They halted in front of the seafood counter. "I'm happy for you," Kyle said, his voice warm and genuine.

Maggie smiled. It felt good to feel this good. Even with the uncertainty of where her relationship with Jarrett was heading, she was feeling better every day. She was actually enjoying life again, hearing music, tasting good food. When Jordan died, Maggie had been sure her life was over, that she would never be more than a walking shell again. She'd been wrong.

She only hoped she could make her relationship with Taylor work. As far as Jarrett was concerned, he was still too great an unknown. Although they had expressed interest in each other, she didn't know if they could make it work.

FOURTEEN

Maggie leaned on the rail of her living room balcony. From here, she could see the ocean to her left and the sun setting over the bay to her right. The breeze had shifted and was coming off the bay, carrying the tangy scent of salt spray and marsh grass.

Maggie liked this time of year, when all the families returned to their homes to prepare for school, leaving the beaches in their more natural state. The nice thing about September was that the air was still warm, the water still tepid.

Maggie heard footsteps behind her. Kyle and Jarrett were in her kitchen washing dishes, talking about some basketball player's salary, so Maggie knew it had to be Taylor coming onto the balcony.

The teen walked to the rail and leaned over. She stood at arm's length from Maggie.

"So how was dinner?" Maggie asked. She knew it had taken a lot of guts for Taylor to step out on the deck alone with her, and she admired her daughter for her courage.

"It was good. Thank you." Her response was a re-action, a product of good manners.

"I'm glad you decided to come."

Taylor gave a snort. "Yeah, right. Like I had a choice. You know my father made me."

Her comment dug deep inside Maggie. It had been a month since she and Jarrett had told Taylor the truth. After this much time, Maggie had thought her relationship with Taylor would have improved, but it hadn't. Her daughter was still being nothing more than civil to her.

"Taylor, I understand why you're so angry with me—"

"You don't understand," Taylor cut in bitterly. "How could you? All these years I thought I was one person and now you're telling me I'm another."

Maggie turned to face her daughter, but Taylor kept her gaze stubbornly averted. "My finding you doesn't change who you are, Taylor. I don't want to take anything from the life you have with your father. I just want to add to it." She softened. "Every girl needs a mother."

"You're not my mother." Taylor stuck out her lower lip. "A mother takes her daughter to the ladies' room at the mall. A mother bakes heart cookies and sends them to class on Valentine's Day. A mother helps her daughter pick out a bra that fits right." She crossed her arms over her chest. "You're not my mother. You never did any of those things. You were nothing but an egg."

"Ouch," Maggie said aloud. "If you meant to hurt me, that one did it."

"I'm sorry," Taylor confessed. "I didn't mean to hurt you, I just—" Tears filled her eyes. "I don't want you to hurt me. I don't want you to hurt my dad."

"Ah, sweetheart." Maggie took a chance and draped one arm over her daughter's shoulder.

Taylor stiffened, but she didn't pull away.

"I'm so sorry for what I did. If I had it to do over again, I never would have let them take you away from me. I'd have found you that very same week."

Taylor wiped at her eyes with her forearm, sniffing. "Dad says he thinks I was taken from you illegally."

Maggie nodded. " 'Fraid so."

"He said your mother made you give me up, that she convinced you it would be best for me, because you couldn't have taken care of me without a college education."

"She made me think giving you up was my only option. I was young and I was scared and I believed her."

"I would never do that to my daughter if she got pregnant," Taylor said, shaking her head.

"Neither would I," Maggie whispered.

"I told my best friend, Heather, that you came to see me."

"Did you?" Maggie smiled, letting her arm slip from her daughter's shoulder. She didn't want to let go of her, not ever, but she didn't want to smother her, either, not when Taylor was finally opening up to her. "And what did Heather say?"

They both leaned on the balcony rail, side by side, just as Maggie imagined a mother and daughter would.

"She didn't say much about my finding out I had a mother who was alive, but she thought it was cool that you're a doctor. She wants to be a doctor, too. She wanted to know if she could ride in your car."

"Yes, she can have a ride." Maggie fiddled with the cuticle of one of her fingers. "So how about you? What do you want to be?"

Taylor shrugged. "I don't know. I used to think I wanted to be an archaeologist, but I love history so much that maybe I'd like to be a teacher. Not for high school, but maybe college."

"You'd make a good teacher."

"What makes you say that?" Taylor dared a hesitant gaze into her mother's eyes. "You don't know me."

Maggie heard the hostility creeping into her daughter's voice again. "I think I do know you. I'm a pretty observant person. I know you're smart, that you express yourself well and that you can be very creative, but you can also appreciate someone else's creativity." She brushed a stray lock of hair behind Taylor's ear. It was silky smooth between her fingers. "And I know you're beautiful."

"Me?" Taylor wrinkled her sun-freckled nose. "Not me. I still look like a little girl. Dad will barely let me wear makeup to school, and all my girlfriends call me Flatso because I don't have any boobs."

Maggie smiled. She remembered the pains of adolescence all too well. "I think your boobs are just right for your size, and you *are* beautiful. You're beautiful to me."

The teen blushed. "You're just saying that because you're my m—" She cut herself off.

"Because I'm your mom?"

Taylor nodded, compressing her lips, the sparkle of tears in her eyes again. There was something else bothering her.

"Taylor, what is it?" Maggie hated seeing her daughter in pain like this. It tore her up inside, especially because Maggie knew she was responsible for all the upheaval. "You can tell me."

She shook her head.

"Oh, come on," Maggie cajoled. "It really is better if we talk. You can tell me you're angry with me. Shoot, you can even tell me you don't like me, if that's it. Just talk to me."

"That's not it," Taylor said, her voice barely audible. "I do like you." She sniffed.

Maggie took a step closer. "Then what is it?"

Taylor looked up at Maggie, her eyes shining with new tears. "Are you going to leave again?"

"Oh, Taylor." Without fear of smothering her, Maggie wrapped her arms around her daughter and hugged her tightly. She felt different than Jordan, but so good in her arms, as if she belonged there. "No, I'm not going to leave you. I did that once and I'll never do it again. I swear I won't."

"OK," Taylor said into Maggie's shoulder, sniffing again. "OK."

Maggie drew back to look into her eyes. "So is this why you've been so cool with me? Because you thought I was just passing through?"

"Dumb, huh?" Taylor took a step back, wiping her tears.

"No." Maggie's brow creased. "Not dumb at all."

"Anyone want coffee or tea out here? Kyle says dessert's almost ready." Jarrett stuck his head through the doorway. He immediately saw Taylor had been crying and looked to Maggie for an explanation.

Taylor spoke up before Maggie could. "I'm fine, Dad. Can I have some coffee? Just half a cup?" She ducked under her father's arm and disappeared into the house.

"Is everything OK?" Jarrett stepped onto the deck.

Maggie rested her elbows on the rail, smiling. "Great. Everything's great. We still need to talk, but I think we've had our breakthrough." She couldn't stop grinning.

"That right?" He leaned on the rail beside her, his arm brushing hers.

Maggie could feel the sexual tension arc between them like static electricity on a stormy night. It had been like this all evening. Was Kyle right? Were she and Jarrett headed for the bedroom?

Was that what she wanted?

"Maggie?"

"Mm-hm?" Suddenly too nervous to look at Jarrett, she stared out at the ocean. He could feel that same sexual tension between them, she just knew it.

"I have to admit I've enjoyed the time we've spent together, you and Taylor and I."

"So have I." She dared a quick glance at him, then focused again on the white ocean breakers.

"And I have to confess secretly I was a little pleased that Taylor was so angry with you and you needed me as a buffer."

"Why?"

He shrugged, his muscles rippling beneath his faded surfer's T-shirt. He'd gotten his hair cut recently, so he didn't look so much like a beach bum, but more like a relaxed kind of guy. "I don't know. I suppose because I got to spend time with you, too."

So this was it—his signal. He was ready to move on to the next stage in the relationship. Was she?

"So is it coming to that?" she asked softly.

"To you and me?" He massaged her shoulder. "I think so. Is that what you want?"

Maggie's gaze met his. "How about you? Are you ready for that? Can you forgive me for being a coward? For letting my mother take our child from me?" Her eyes grew scratchy, but she fought her tears. She wanted to be able to talk about this without crying. It was time to stop crying and get on with life. Taylor was proof that there was still so much here for her, that God hadn't abandoned her. "Can you forgive me for being too big a coward to come looking for her, *for you?*"

He squeezed her arm. "That depends on whether you can forgive me for doing what I did with Lisa, for taking Taylor and not trying too awfully hard to find you, for being so damned angry with you all these years and wanting you at the same time. I was as big a coward as you were."

"Oh, Jarrett." She turned to face him. "I think it's too late."

His face fell. "Too late?"

She dared a tiny smile. "Too late because at some point over the past few weeks, I realized I already had forgiven you."

Jarrett lowered his mouth to hers and she lifted on her toes to meet him. The shape of his lips, the taste of his tongue were so familiar and still so arousing.

How many times had she dreamed of his kisses? Now that he was kissing her again, she wanted it to go on forever.

They parted, both breathless, and he pressed a kiss to her forehead. "We can take it slow. As slow as you need," he said, his voice husky with desire for her.

Maggie almost laughed aloud. She was moving slowly all right, like a freight train. There she had been, her groin molded to his, her tongue in his mouth, her fingernails digging into his back. It had been so long since she'd felt this passionate with any man. The truth was no man had ever excited her as Jarrett did.

Maggie was ready to move on. She felt stronger, more sure of herself than she had since Stanley's and Jordan's deaths, maybe longer. She and Jarrett and Taylor had a lot of issues to mull over, but she really felt as if they were making progress. There was only one nagging detail about the past that was still unanswered.

Maggie bit down on her lower lip. "Jarrett, can I ask you something?"

"Sure." He toyed with her hair. He looked so happy. "Fire away."

"How did you know I had Taylor? How did you know I was in Tucson? How did you get her so soon after she was born? Who told you?"

He stiffened, releasing her hair. "Do we really need to go into this? I already said I forgive you. You forgive me. Taylor needs us to be here for her now, not in the past."

Maggie was tempted to let it go again, but she couldn't. "Jarrett, I have to know how you knew I was pregnant when you were in Spain."

His intense blue eyes met hers. "I think you already know."

She shook her head. Somewhere deep inside, maybe she did, but she wasn't ready to admit it, not even to herself. She wasn't ready to believe in that kind of betrayal.

"Sure you do." His voice took on an angry edge. "Tell me."

"No."

She stared at him incredulously. "No?"

"Look, it's late. We've got to be going."

She grabbed his shoulder as he turned away. "You can't just say no and walk away."

"Sure I can." He stepped through the doorway. "Taylor, grab your things, hon. Time to go home."

"But we haven't had dessert yet, Dad," came their daughter's voice from the kitchen.

"You said you wanted to spend the night with Heather. If you're going to, it's now or never."

Maggie stood on the deck, her arms crossed in disbelief as Jarrett disappeared into the house. "Damn you," she whispered under her breath. Part of her wanted to go after him, but part of her wanted to let him go.

Tonight they had come so close to the beginning of a relationship, and then this. She turned her back to the house, fighting anger and hurt. Maybe it was better this way. Maybe it just wasn't meant to be.

"Place stationary bottom shelf between sides A and B, finish out, and fasten with rods," Jarrett read aloud.

He sat cross-legged on the floor in front of his couch, bookcase shelves scattered around him. He dumped a bag of screws onto the carpet. "Rods? What rods? What the hell is a rod?" He let both sides of the bookcase go and they fell noisily onto the pile, nicking his toe as they went down. "Ouch!" He massaged the injured digit. "I've got a master's degree and I can't understand these directions. How is anyone else going to?" he muttered angrily.

It was almost midnight. Ordinarily he would have been in bed by now, but he hadn't been able to sleep. Taylor had gone to spend the night at Heather's, so he was left alone to pace the house. First he'd tried reading, but nothing held his attention, not even the latest high-tech thriller he'd bought at the bookstore, so he'd decided to do a little work.

He had employees who put the products together using directions other employees wrote, but he still liked to put furniture together himself on occasion for quality control.

Irritated, Jarrett got up off the floor and walked to the kitchen to get something to drink. He opened the fridge. His choice was skim milk or red Kool-Aid. Deciding he wasn't so thirsty after all, he let the door swing shut, leaving the kitchen in darkness again.

Maybe he ought to call Maggie. He shouldn't have left her house in anger. He wasn't angry with her, but he knew he'd left that impression—and just when it seemed they were about to bridge that gap between them, just when they might have a chance.

Jarrett could still taste Maggie's sweet lips on his. He could close his eyes and feel her touch. She made him feel so alive and good inside—good about himself. She made him feel young again, like he could do anything or be anything.

"Just call her," he mumbled to himself. "Tell her you're sorry."

But then he would have to answer her question. He would have to tell the truth, and he didn't want to be the one to do it. He wasn't even sure he had a right to.

Still, he knew he wouldn't be able sleep until he talked to her. Before he could chicken out, Jarrett picked up the cordless phone from its cradle on the kitchen wall. Just as he punched the first number, he heard a knock on the back door.

FIFTEEN

The door swung open and Maggie smiled hesitantly. "Hi."

Jarrett grinned, obviously glad to see her and seeming not the least bit surprised. He was still wearing his shorts and T-shirt, but he was barefoot, looking rumpled and all the sexier for his dishevelment. Apparently he, too, had tried to sleep but couldn't. He held the phone in his hand.

"Calling someone this late?" She lifted one eyebrow. She knew he was calling her. She'd just beaten him to the apology.

She walked into the living room, brushing past his warmth, already feeling better. That was the great thing about old friends—they knew you so well, and you knew them so well.

"Maggie I'm sorry I left like that." Jarrett dropped the phone on the counter and ran one hand through his sun-bleached hair. "I wasn't angry with you. Only with the situation."

"I know." She gazed at his bare feet, feeling a little awkward with the subject. "It was my fault," she said. "I shouldn't have cornered you like that. You were right. I do know the answer. I . . . just didn't want to admit it." She fought the lump rising in her throat.

"Aw, Maggie, I'm sorry," Jarrett whispered.

He pulled her into his arms, and she went willingly.

"Even after everything she did," Maggie whispered, "I didn't want to believe it." She buried her face in Jarrett's shoulder, breathing deeply, enveloping herself in the scent of fabric softener and his maleness. "I wanted to believe that she really did love me on some level."

"Oh, Maggie." He angled back and gazed into her eyes. "She did love you. She does. In her way."

Maggie shook her head, still fighting tears. "No mother could love her child and do what she did."

"She thought she was doing the right thing," he said firmly. "She didn't want you to end up the way she had—uneducated, with a dead-end job, getting old before your time."

Maggie pressed her cheek to Jarrett's shoulder again. Her mother had gotten pregnant out of wedlock with Lisa. Maggie's father wasn't Lisa's father. She'd always known it, although no one had ever said it. Ruth had married Bob, The Bread Man, so she'd have a wedding ring on her finger when the baby came. Ruth had put Taylor up for adoption to save her daughter from the pain she herself had gone through. It wasn't right, but she had done the best she could at the time.

"And in a way, she was looking out for Taylor's best interests, too," he said quietly. "She contacted my parents because she thought our daughter would be better off with grandparents than strangers. I'm sure she never guessed I would be the one to take Taylor."

Maggie rubbed her cheek against Jarrett's soft T-shirt. It was damp where a few of her tears had spilled. "Then your parents told you and you flew home to the States?"

"Got an apartment and a babysitter. Raised our daughter," he said, smoothing her hair.

"Thank you," Maggie whispered, truly grateful to the very tips of her toes. "Maybe Mother was right. Maybe I couldn't have cared for her."

"I don't believe that, not for one minute."

"I should talk to her."

"You *should* talk to her. You've put it off long enough."

"You'll go with me?"

"I'll go with you. I told you that. This weekend, if you like. Taylor will be with Heather all weekend. They went to her grandfather's farm in Dover. She won't be home until Monday sometime around lunch."

She glanced up, smiling through the tears she'd sworn she wouldn't shed. "I could love you, Jarrett McKay. I could love you so easily," she murmured huskily.

"I already love you. Never stopped loving you."

As Jarrett brushed his lips against Maggie's, she knew everything would be all right. She knew she and Jarrett would fall in love all over again, knew they already had. And she knew she, Jarrett, and Taylor could make a life together. A good life.

Jarrett lifted Maggie into his arms and she laughed, throwing her head back, looping her arms around his neck. "You're just too romantic for words," she whispered, covering his face with kisses as he carried her down the hall to his bedroom.

A desk lamp softly illuminated the cozy room. He carried her to the tumbled, slept-in sheets of his king-size bed and laid her down gently.

"This is almost like the first time," she whispered, smiling and not even a little bit self-conscious. "Remember? In your room when your parents weren't home?"

He pulled his T-shirt over his head, revealing his sun-bronzed, muscular chest. "Let's hope I can last a little longer than that."

She laughed as she kicked off her sandals and pulled her T-shirt over her head. She was braless, so there was nowhere to hide.

But this was Jarrett—her Jarrett, who had held her in his arms so many times. Her Jarrett, who had made her sandcastles and kissed her until she was weak in the knees in the front seat of his red Mustang. She didn't want to hide.

"So beautiful," he whispered as he climbed into bed, his hand brushing the curve of one of her breasts. He stretched his hard form over her softer, more rounded one, and gazed deep into her eyes.

"Can't tell you how many times I've dreamed of this." His lips brushed hers.

"Me, too." She drew a line along his lower lip with the tip of her tongue. "Just without the stretch marks."

His hand spanned the flat plane of her abdomen and he bent to kiss her navel. "Makes you more beautiful to me. Proof of our love and our love for Taylor."

Maggie threaded her fingers through his thick hair

and tugged gently. "Come here," she whispered, "where I can see you."

He stretched out beside her in the tangle of sheets so he could touch and be touched.

They kissed, they stroked. They reminisced and they reached out to create new memories, discover new responses, heightened pleasures. Within seconds, Maggie's body was alive with sensation. Within minutes, she burned with a desire fiercer than she remembered.

As Maggie's breath came quicker, the urgency inside her intensified, and she wondered if all of the pain she had experienced had enabled her to feel pleasure more profoundly.

Their bare arms and legs entwined, they merged in a coming together of the past and the future.

As Jarrett rose and fell above her, driving her further and further toward the precipice, she called out his name in the darkness.

"Maggie, Maggie." He smothered her with hot, wet kisses, lifting her higher, faster.

Jarrett's warm breath, his name on her lips, the comfort, the passion of feeling him deep inside her pushed her over the edge. She crashed with a great tensing of muscles and the fiery white light of fulfillment.

Maggie's cries of ecstasy brought Jarrett home close behind her. A moment later, they were lying in each other's arms, panting and laughing. For once Maggie had no tears, only a satisfied grin.

"Wow," Jarrett whispered.

She giggled. She really did feel seventeen again. "Yeah, wow."

Then Jarrett pulled the sheet over them both, and

they slept in each other's arms in complete peace, maybe for the first time since they'd parted all those years ago.

Maggie adjusted her sunglasses, staring straight ahead, the wind whipping at her ponytail. Jarrett, behind the wheel of her car, reached over and patted her knee.

"Nervous?" he asked.

She grimaced. "I feel like I could puke."

He cracked a grin. "Oh, come on. Things are never as bad as you imagine they'll be."

"Ha! You don't know Ruth. She is not an open-up-and-share-your-feelings kind of gal. I walk up to her and say 'Mom, why'd you give my baby away?' and she might kick us both out the screen door." She glanced out the open window and watched the telephone poles fly by. "Or she might give such a reasonable explanation that we walk out of there thinking she might have done the right thing."

"You and I both know she had no right to do what she did. No matter what she says or how she tries to justify her actions, she was wrong, Maggie. She was wrong and she needs to know it. She needs to hear it from you." He covered her hand on the seat with his. "But no matter what she says, at least you'll have confronted her. Maybe you can find some peace, even if she can't."

Maggie closed her eyes. She really did feel sick to her stomach now. Maybe it was the passing poles making her motion sick, or maybe it was just the thought of talking to Ruth about Taylor. "I know I need to do this. I'm just not looking forward to it."

"What you can look forward to is a night with me." He glanced sideways at her as he returned his hand to the wheel. "I made reservations at a little inn on the Chesapeake. We'll check out a few antique shops, I'll buy you an ice cream cone, we'll have dinner by the water, and then . . ." His tone grew low and sexy.

"And then?" She couldn't resist a smile. How had she lived without him all these years? He could always make her smile.

"And then you might get lucky, lady."

She laughed, and somehow knew no matter how horrendous her meeting with her mother might be, Jarrett would help her get through it.

"Want iced tea?" Ruth asked nervously, hovering in the archway between the kitchen and the living room.

She was dressed for work in a white polyester nurse's aide uniform, her leather shoes streaked with white shoe polish.

Maggie had offered again and again to buy her mother colored smocks for work; everyone at the hospital wore them these days. They were so much cheerier than the stark white. But Ruth refused. Dingy white polyester was what she wore because it was what she had always worn. The eleventh commandment: Thou shalt not instill change in thy dress or manner. Ever.

Maggie hadn't told her mother she was bringing

Jarrett. Needless to say, Ruth was shocked to see him after all these years. Shocked, but not shocked enough to ask her daughter why he was here—why either of them was here, for that matter. Ruth lived by the don't-ask-questions-you-don't-want-the-answers-to rule.

Jarrett sat on the edge of a couch covered in a slip-cover that sported limes and lemons. "Iced tea would be nice, thank you. With lemon."

"Don't have lemon." Ruth fussed with her hair. Her roots were showing. Maggie had offered to pay to have her mother's hair professionally colored monthly, too, but she refused. Miss Clairol was what she had always used.

Jarrett leaned back and smiled. Maggie could tell it was forced. "Plain tea will be fine, thank you."

Too nervous to sit, Maggie stood near the TV cabinet. The TV was on, the volume down low. Her father was asleep in his easy chair. A game show was on the tube; contestants jumped up and down as their names were called.

Ruth didn't offer Maggie tea, and Maggie didn't ask for any. They both knew she would bring it to her whether she wanted it or not.

"Lisa was here last weekend," Ruth called from the kitchen. "She bought a new car. They say it won some kind of award last year. Nice car. Air and power windows."

Maggie had to press her lips together to keep from calling out, "Ma, all new cars have air conditioning and power windows."

"The MacGrogens next door are taking a bus tour to Maine." Ice cubes popped out of a tray and rattled onto the kitchen counter. "They say it's beautiful up there in the fall. Lots of leaves."

Maggie ground her teeth. How many times in her life had she heard Ruth tell her what *they* said? Maggie still didn't know who the hell *they* were.

Maggie leaned on the pressed fiber TV cabinet and absently wondered if Jarrett's company had written the directions for its assembly. She pressed her finger and thumb to her temples. It was hot in the house. Ruth had oscillating fans placed around the room, but all they seemed to do was push the hot air around.

"Ma, why don't you turn on the air conditioner?" Maggie had had central air installed several years ago because her father's emphysema was worse in the heat. Ruth rarely used it. Her father suffered in silence, as he always had.

"It's not so hot." She came to the doorway with iced tea in two flowered glasses. "Besides, the electric is high enough."

Maggie looked to Jarrett for moral support. He smiled, and that smile gave her the courage to go on. She took the glasses of tea from her mother and passed one to Jarrett. She placed the other on the coffee table littered with women's magazines. "Ma, I need to talk to you."

Ruth stood in the doorway, glancing uneasily in Jarrett's direction. "I have to go to work soon."

"You don't have to be at work until four. It's only one."

"Yeah, but I have to stop at the store. Your father's out of nasal spray and we're out of toilet paper. Your father likes their economy brand there. He says it's softer than any of those name brands."

Maggie closed her eyes for a second, breathing deeply. Her heart was racing. "Ma, will you sit down?" She indicated the opposite end of the couch from where Jarrett sat.

Ruth crossed her arms and leaned against the doorway. "I'm fine standing," she said, digging in as a soldier readies for battle.

Maggie met her mother's gaze. She knew those tired hazel eyes so well, and yet at this moment she felt as if she didn't know her mother at all—never had known her. "I guess you're wondering what Jarrett's doing here with me," she started awkwardly.

She lifted a sagging shoulder. "I try not to get into my grown daughters' business."

"Ma, didn't you ever wonder how she was?" Maggie said suddenly, opening her arms in a plea.

Ruth stared blankly. "Who?"

"My *daughter.*" Maggie choked on the word.

Jarrett rose, leaving his untouched tea on the coffee table. He draped one arm over Maggie's shoulder in a comforting squeeze.

Ruth stared at the floor. "I always knew you'd throw that up in my face," she said bitterly. "I did what I thought was right at the time. It's all a parent can do."

Maggie had to look away. Her gaze fell on her father in his recliner. He was overweight, with sagging jowls and a nearly bald head ringed by gray hair. He still wore the blue uniform work pants and shirt he had worn all his life, only now that he had retired, the bread company logo was gone. He slept on.

Maggie turned back to her mother. "You took my baby, Ma. Without my permission. You took her out of my arms and you put her up for adoption without my signature. That's illegal."

"What would you have done with a baby?" she snapped. "You in college? You were going to be a doctor! How do you think you would have gotten through medical school with a preschooler under your feet? Huh?" She pointed her finger. "Well, I can tell you. You wouldn't have!"

"So maybe I wouldn't have become a physician. Would that have been so bad? Would that have been such a terrible trade-off?" Maggie could feel her face burning with anger. "A child for a medical degree?"

Her mother drew her thin lips back, crossing her arms over her lumpy chest again. "It wasn't what I wanted for you. You deserved better."

Maggie exhaled and lowered her voice, softening her tone. This was pointless. She had known it would be pointless. Ruth was never going to see what she had done wrong, not if she hadn't recognized it after all these years. "I just think I should have been able to make a choice, that I should have been given some other options."

"You wouldn't have understood what you were giving up. It wasn't what I wanted for you," her mother repeated.

She glanced up at her mother. "So why contact Jarrett's family? Why didn't you just put her up for adoption in Arizona?"

Ruth was silent.

"Ma?"

"College was expensive. You had to have books and meal tickets. Medical school is outrageous."

Maggie felt sick in the pit of her stomach again. What was her mother saying? "Mother, you only paid for undergrad. I borrowed money for medical school. I'm still paying loans."

"Your sister got into some trouble while you were off getting your degree. Rehab doesn't come cheap, you know, not good rehab. They say you have to get a decent place if—"

"You took money for my baby?" Maggie asked incredulously. She looked from her mother to Jarrett. He seemed as startled as she was.

"I never knew," he whispered under his breath.

Maggie looked back at Ruth, who still stood in the doorway. "Did the McKays pay you for my daughter?"

"Legal expenses," she said, waving one hand as if she could dismiss the whole thing. "Court costs. Plane tickets here and there."

Maggie felt herself trembling from head to foot. "You paid for my sister's rehab with money from the sale of my child?"

"I didn't sell any child," Ruth snapped. "I did what I had to do to get my daughters raised. Now if there's nothing else you need, I've got to get ready for work."

Maggie watched, stunned, as Ruth went down the hall and disappeared into the back of the bungalow. Slowly she turned to look at Jarrett.

"I'm so sorry," he said softly. "My parents never

told me they paid her off. They only said she had contacted them to ask if they wanted to adopt the child, saying she couldn't afford to keep her. My parents were under the impression you didn't want her, either."

Tears slid down Maggie's cheeks. "She doesn't even know she did anything wrong."

Jarrett wrapped her in his arms, pulling her close.

"She didn't even ask how Taylor was," Maggie said, feeling almost numb now. Numb was good. "She didn't ask about her granddaughter."

"Shhh," Jarrett soothed. "It's all right, Maggie. It's going to be all right."

Maggie rested her forehead on his shoulder, dampening his shirt with her tears. "Can we go now? I just want to go."

"Sure, sweetheart." He pressed a kiss to her pale, sweaty forehead and ushered her toward the door. "I think we've had enough confrontation for one day."

Maggie lay in the crook of Jarrett's arm, her cheek pressed into his shoulder, her hand on his flat abdomen. The inn he had chosen was perfect, their room cozy and private.

They were both breathing hard, spent from making love. She turned her head and pressed a kiss to his warm skin. "Thanks," she said.

"Well, you're certainly welcome." He chuckled, sliding his hand over her bare buttocks. "I'm glad you enjoyed yourself."

She laughed and smacked him playfully on his stom-

ach. "Not for that." She smiled. "Well, OK, for that.
But I meant for going to my mother's with me."

He scratched her back. "I'm not sure she gave you
a whole lot of satisfaction."

"No, it was all right. In all these years we never
spoke of it at all. At least now it's out. Maybe once
she gets used to the fact, she might even ask about
Taylor."

"Maybe." He was quiet for a minute. "So what do
we tell Taylor about Ruth? The truth?"

Maggie sighed. "I don't know. Let's think about it.
I don't want her to hate her grandmother. I don't want
her to find out we've been dishonest with her again,
either, though. As it is, a certain amount of trust needs
to be rebuilt."

"Maybe we should wait and see what she wants to
know," Jarrett mused, sliding his hand up and down her
arm. "Kids seem to have a way of only asking questions with answers they can handle."

Maggie nodded. "Works for me. One step at a time."

"What about Lisa?"

"What about her?" Maggie still felt prickly discuss-
ing Lisa with Jarrett, but it was getting easier. The
wound was definitely healing.

"Are you going to ask her about rehab? About the
money?"

"No, she said thoughtfully. "I don't think I will.
I'm sure Lisa doesn't know how Ruth paid for her
rehab, otherwise she would have told me. So what's
the point? She's already got enough things to be neurotic about."

"Good point. You're a wise woman, Maggie Turner." He gazed into her eyes. "A kind one, too."

Grinning, she rolled onto his chest, pressing her body against his. He felt so right, so good. "Hush," she whispered. "And let me ravish you."

His eyes twinkled. "Ravish away." He opened his arms in surrender. "I'm all yours."

SIXTEEN

"So tell me about your job," Jarrett said, pulling a rake through the wood chips in the flower bed.

Maggie stood beside him in the side yard of his house, watering a blooming hibiscus. She watched the water spray from the nozzle. "What about it?"

"You like it?"

She smiled. They had driven back from the inn after lunch, but both had been hesitant to end the weekend. Despite the emotion involved in visiting Ruth, it had been a good one. Somehow, by sharing the pain Maggie felt, she and Jarrett came home feeling closer. It was scary, but it felt so good, so right, like the two of them in bed. "I love my job," she said, moving onto the next flowering bush. "It can be exciting. It can also be boring," she admitted. "But I like being able to help people. I like being able to use my knowledge to make them feel better."

He smoothed the wood chip mulch with the rake. "I always knew you'd become a doctor. Knew you'd make a good one, too."

She glanced at him. "What made you think so?"

"You're so compassionate. You feel so deeply. That could only make you a better doctor."

She nodded thoughtfully. "I like to heal the whole patient. Even though I'm in emergency medicine and I only see my patients for a short time, I like to think I see them as whole people and not as broken arms or foot lacerations."

"Well, next time I break an arm or cut my foot, you'll be the doc I ask for."

She turned the hose on him and sprayed a wet path across the back of his T-shirt.

"Hey!" he hollered, jumping out of the way.

She laughed and returned the spray to the flower bed. "Just checking to be sure you're awake."

"Very funny." He dragged the rake through the bed one more time and then stepped back. "There. That's enough yard work for one day—don't you think?" He looked at her. "What say we have a little dinner?"

She dropped the hose and walked over to turn it off at the faucet. "You're not tired of me yet? Not ready to send me home?"

He leaned the rake against the cedar shakes of the house and came to her, his arms open. "No way. You sick of me?"

She walked into his arms and sighed at the feel of them closing around her. "No way."

He kissed the top of her head. "Hungry? Want to go out and get something to eat?"

She gazed up at him. She was so happy she felt as if she needed to pinch herself to see if she was dreaming. There had been discussions of the future. Maggie didn't know for sure where they were headed, but she was hopeful. That was the greatest gift Jarrett MacKay had brought when he'd entered her life again—hope. And no matter what, she knew she would always be indebted to him for it.

"I'm hungry," she said, smiling because he made her feel like smiling. "Steamed blue claws would be great."

"Crabs?" He nodded. "I could pick a few crabs. I know a good place to get them. Picnic tables, cement floor they can hose down, flypaper hanging from the ceiling."

She laughed. "Do they steam for takeout?"

"I imagine they do. Why? You want to just eat here?"

"Whatever you want. I was thinking we could pull a table out on the deck, eat, and then maybe go for a swim. You always used to like to swim at night."

"That was because I could put my hands in your bikini top without anyone seeing me," he teased.

"Maybe that could be arranged, as well."

He brushed the hair that fell over her forehead, still holding her in his arms. "Want to stay the night?"

"I can stay a while, but I should go home. Taylor will be back tomorrow, and I don't think she's ready to see us together like this. Besides, I have work in the morning."

"Taylor won't be home until lunch time. As far as us, she's a smart girl. I think she's beginning to suspect."

Maggie smoothed the nape of his neck. "I suppose we're getting along rather well for a couple supposedly battling over custody."

"She's known enough girlfriends' divorcing parents

to know most ex-couples don't get along as well as we do." He dropped his arms from her waist, grabbed her hand, and led her around the corner of the house. "But I still think we need to take it slowly. Let her get used to the idea."

Maggie wanted to ask what idea. Did he mean them as a couple? But she wasn't ready to ask, maybe because she wasn't ready for the answer yet. "How do you think she's going to react when she does find out?"

"I would think she'd be pleased."

"You would think," Maggie echoed.

"On the other hand, she *is* a teenager."

Maggie chuckled. "You're right. Enough said."

They started up the steps, Maggie ahead of him. "I'll call for the crabs," he said. "You see if you can find the mallets. Deal?"

"Deal."

"And you'll stay with me tonight? Sleep in my arms?" he asked.

At the top of the flight of stairs she halted and turned to face him. Standing on the deck with him one step below put them eye to eye. She leaned forward and kissed him. "I'll stay," she said.

He winked. "I promise I'll make it worth your while."

She turned away. "I know you will. Why else would I be staying?" she called over her shoulder.

They laughed together in the fading afternoon light.

Maggie woke to the sound of Taylor's voice. For a moment she thought she was still dreaming.

"Dad, aren't you up yet?"

Maggie opened her eyes drowsily and then closed them again. Sunlight poured through the half-open drapes, drowning Jarrett's bed in warmth.

Jarrett's bed!

She came fully awake, her eyes snapping open. Jarrett lay sound asleep on his stomach, one arm draped over her hips.

"Jar—"

His name wasn't out of Maggie's mouth before Taylor appeared in the doorway. "Dad, do you know where my—"

Maggie's gaze met her daughter's. Taylor's jaw dropped. Maggie and Jarrett were both naked and only partially covered by a sheet. Instinctively Maggie pulled the sheet up to cover her bare breasts.

"What are you doing here?" Taylor demanded.

Maggie elbowed Jarrett, trying to wake him. Her eyes were scratchy and she was having a hard time focusing.

"Now, Taylor—" Maggie sat up in bed, gripping the sheet firmly.

"Don't try to tell me this isn't what I think." Taylor snapped. "Don't even try it." She dropped one hand to her slender hip. "I guess this is why you've been coming around, isn't it? To get my father back, not for me."

Maggie was shocked speechless by Taylor's words. Before she could form a reasonable thought, Taylor was gone, running down the hall.

"Oh, hell," Maggie muttered.

"Oh, hell," Jarrett echoed sleepily.

Maggie looked down to see Jarrett open his eyes. He

rolled to his back, pulling the sheet from her as he moved.

"Guess you caught that, huh?"

"Maybe not in its entirety, but enough."

The back door shut with a resounding slam. Something fell off the wall and hit the floor with a clatter.

"I'm sorry," Maggie said. "I never heard her let herself in. I was sound asleep."

"You're sorry? What do you have to be sorry about?" He rubbed his eyes. "She wasn't supposed to be home until noon. She was clear on that when she left."

Maggie had to laugh, though she was far from amused. "I can't believe this." She slid down in the bed until her head was on the pillow again. The sheets smelled wonderfully of him and her and last night's lovemaking. "This is worse than being caught by our parents." She pulled the sheet over her head.

He chuckled and yanked the sheet off, tossing it to the floor. "Ah, this is more like it." He placed a warm kiss between her breasts.

"Jarrett, shouldn't we go after her? She's really upset." She pushed his head away.

With a groan he sat up. "I guess you're right. I'm sure she just went down on the beach to cool off. She always does when she's upset with me."

"I would say this is a little more than upset." Maggie slid to the edge of the bed in search of her discarded clothes. "Want me to go find her?"

He rose from the bed and walked toward the master bath. "Let's get dressed, put the coffeepot on—or tea, for those who prefer it—and then find her together."

He flashed a smile over his shoulder and Maggie melted inside. He was so handsome naked, all sinew and muscle and suntan lines. She liked him disheveled from making love.

"Tea," she agreed. "Definitely tea." Then she remembered work. How could she have forgotten work? "Oh, no. What time is it?" She glanced around his still unfamiliar bedroom, looking for the clock.

"Ten after seven."

"Oh, great. My daughter's caught me naked in bed with her father *and* I'm late for work." She jumped out of bed and pulled on a T-shirt she recovered from the tangle of the cotton blanket on the floor.

"Guess we'll have to start earlier tonight." He winked and disappeared into the bathroom.

By the time he was out, she had dressed and called Talbany General ER to let someone know she was running late. One of the other physicians said he'd be happy to cover for her until she arrived, but she felt guilty for sleeping in. "Listen, I need to get home to change and get to work," she told Jarrett. "Should we go find Taylor now?"

He gave her a peck on the cheek. "Nah. I haven't dated much. Done even less of *this,*" he admitted, gesturing to the bed. "And then only without her knowledge, so she's probably just as upset about realizing I'm a man and not just a dad as the fact that I was with you. Let me get my coffee and go down to the beach. I'll talk to her. Maybe we can meet you for a quick lunch or dinner if you're not too busy. Give her time to cool down."

Maggie rested her hand on the doorjamb of the bathroom. "You don't think she really thinks my attention to her was meant to get at you, do you?"

"Honestly?" He pulled on his shorts without bothering with his boxers. "Probably not. Well, maybe just a little. I told you, teenagers can come up with some crazy ideas. But Taylor has always gone for the drama of a scene. She likes to make more of issues than are there. She likes to exaggerate her own feelings, maybe just to try them out." He gave a wave. "Once she gets used to the idea, she'll be fine."

"OK," Maggie said hesitantly. "If that's what you think. Just promise me that after you talk to her, you'll call me at work and let me know how she is."

He pulled his T-shirt over his head. "You don't think I could go all day without talking to you, do you?"

He was still grinning at her with that sexy smile of his when she closed the bathroom door.

Jarrett left Maggie a message around eleven in the morning, but she was busy until after lunch with a pop-top laceration, a family with a suspected case of slight salmonella poisoning, two sprained ankles, and a suspected MI. It wasn't until almost one that she finally had the time to grab a soda in the physician's lounge and make a personal phone call.

"Hello," came Jarrett's voice over the phone.

"Hi, there." She couldn't resist a smile as she remembered flashes of last night's lovemaking. "How's our favorite daughter doing? Is she really upset with us? Packing her bags to join the Foreign Legion?"

He paused. It wasn't until that moment that Maggie realized his greeting had been strained. "Jarrett?"

"Maggie, she's not here. I'm getting worried."

"Not there?" She set down her soda can. A tiny current of fear curled up her spine. "What do you mean she's not there? She's not there with you? She went back to Heather's?"

"I mean she's not here. I can't find her. She's not on the beach. She's not at Heather's. They dropped her off early because Heather had to change her flute lesson time. No one's seen Taylor."

"Have you called the police?"

"I think I'm going to now. It's been six hours. I know she's almost fifteen, so I gave her as much time as I could, but I think I have to do it." His voice was tight with concern. "I know she's a responsible young woman, but this just isn't like her. She wouldn't just take off. She knows how much I worry about her safety. She's old enough to be aware of what kind of world we live in."

Maggie jumped out of her chair. "I'll be right there."

SEVENTEEN

"My father is going to be pissed when he figures out I'm gone!" Taylor shouted from the shadowy basement room her kidnappers had locked her in. She kicked the solid wooden door once with her toe; then, in frustration, she turned and slammed it with the heel of her tennis shoe. "And you won't like it when you see how pissed he can get."

"Shut up in there!" came an agitated male voice from the other side of the door. "You hear me? Shut up, or I'll use duct tape on that mouth of yours."

Taylor crossed her arms over her chest angrily, but she didn't speak again. She wasn't afraid of having her mouth taped so much as having to face her kidnappers again. At least alone in this awful room, she felt a little safe.

But the minute she turned away from the door, her brief fit of anger subsided into terror again. She paced the tiny, dark room, tears running down her face. How could this be happening to her? Real kids didn't get kidnapped, not kids like her who got good grades and tried to do what her father asked her to. That was just in movies, wasn't it?

A sob escaped her and she clamped her hand over her mouth to keep the men from hearing her.

Why was this happening to her? She had done everything right when the men grabbed her in the alley at the end of her street down near the beach. She did everything her dad and guidance counselors at school had said to do if someone tried to snatch you. She hollered, she kicked, she screamed.

But no one heard her. No one saw them slap her so hard that she went dizzy. No one saw them throw her into the beat-up old utility van and take off.

She wiped her runny nose with the sleeve of the sweatshirt emblazoned with the name of her father's alma mater. She was so scared she was trembling all over. Her stomach was so upset she felt like she was going to barf, only she hadn't had any breakfast.

"What am I going to do? What am I going to do?" she whispered over and over again in a chant. "Daddy, Daddy, what do I do?"

She was never the kind of person who got really upset over things. She had always taken pride in the fact she could stay calm even when people got hurt, like the time Heather fell off her horse at the stable and broke her arm. But Taylor could feel herself losing control. She was almost hysterical.

"OK," she murmured, hugging herself. "OK, I gotta stay calm. This isn't going to help."

She took a few deep breaths, trying to make her heart stop pounding so hard that it hurt her chest. "Dad says you have to stay calm in bad situations."

Taylor didn't know where she was, but she didn't think she was more than half an hour from home. That's how long she thought it had taken to get here. She didn't know much more than that. The van had had no windows in the back and they had blindfolded her before dragging her into this house, down the basement steps, and into the windowless room.

There was nothing in her prisonlike cell but an old mattress, a floor lamp without a shade, and a Porta-potty like the ones you took camping. She scrunched up her nose. She'd have to pee pretty bad to use that. There were no windows, a concrete floor, and only one door. She could hear an occasional car outside, but she could tell she wasn't on a major road.

Her kidnappers were watching TV on the other side of the door. There were only two. One was called Cal. He was the one who'd just hollered at her, the one in charge. He had greasy blond hair and a scar above her eyebrow. He wore a torn Def Leppard T-shirt. She remembered that because she liked Def Leppard.

The other man was named Ants. He wasn't as rough as Cal and had tried to make her more comfortable on the floor in the back of the van on the way here. He told her not to be afraid. He was the one who had helped her duck so she wouldn't hit her head going down the steps to the basement, blindfolded.

Taylor took another couple of deep breaths, feeling better. Calmer. She had no doubt her father would find her. Right now he and Maggie were looking for her. They had cops and dogs and helicopters aiding the search. With any luck at all, she wouldn't have to pee before they got here, broke in the door, and arrested her kidnappers.

Taylor pushed back her tangled hair. OK. So where

were the police, the dogs, her father, and Maggie? Her chest tightened again and tears filled her eyes.

"No, no," she whispered. "Gotta stay calm. Gotta think about something else. Think about school starting. Think about Dad and Maggie."

Dad and Maggie . . .

This was all Taylor's fault; she knew that. If she hadn't acted so stupid about seeing her father and Maggie naked together, it wouldn't have happened in the first place. Here she was trying to convince her dad how grown-up and mature she was, and then she pulled a stupid stunt like this.

Her friend Heather would give anything to have her parents get back together again. Taylor didn't know why she'd reacted like that when she saw the two of them in bed. Taylor really did like Maggie.

They were alike in so many ways, and Maggie was so smart and so funny. And the best thing was, she made Dad smile—no, she made him grin like one of those goofy high school boys she knew. When Maggie was around, he was always grinning.

Taylor still didn't understand exactly what had happened between her parents before she was born, but she was beginning to think they had made a big mistake in breaking up. Even if they were young, they must have loved each other an awful lot to still be in love after all these years.

And now maybe Taylor had ruined everything. She had said that awful thing to Maggie. She knew it wasn't really true. She knew Maggie hadn't been trying to get her father back through her. In the beginning, Maggie had even avoided her father.

Maybe she'd said it because a part of her wanted to have her father and her mother to herself. She didn't want to share either of them with the other. Now it sounded stupid even thinking about it. She wasn't dumb enough to think the entire world revolved around her, or that she could be solely responsible for her father's happiness. Taylor plopped down on the mattress on the floor. Well, she couldn't fix anything with Maggie and her dad unless she got out of here. *Until* she got out of here. Right now she just had to stay calm and wait.

"I'm sorry, Mr. McKay. I understand your concern, but she *is* a teenage girl, and teenage girls have been known to run away. It's my job to ask."

Jarrett, Maggie, and a Talbany Beach police officer stood in the middle of Jarrett's living room. Maggie had offered the officer a seat, but he had declined.

"Understand my concern!" Jarrett exploded. "The hell you understand my concern. My daughter did not run away. She has never been late to dinner in her life, never missed the school bus, never gone home with a friend without checking with me first. I'm telling you this is not like her. *Something* has happened."

"Jarrett, we need to stay calm," Maggie said, brushing his forearm.

She was as upset as he was, maybe more so, because she knew from experience that when a person thought *this can't happen to me,* it did happen. But someone had to stay calm, and right now it was apparently her turn. She couldn't go to pieces because Taylor needed her and Jarrett needed her. She couldn't think of all the terrible things that could have happened to Taylor; that wouldn't help, either. And she certainly couldn't contemplate what her life would be like if she found her daughter after all these years only to lose her to tragedy. She wouldn't think about it. She just wouldn't.

"I'm not an idiot," Jarrett continued. "I own a large corporation and I realize I could be the target of something like this. We have certain rules in this household, and my daughter abides by them."

The officer waited calmly until Jarrett finished. "Sir, I'll file your daughter's report. Our patrolmen in cars as well as on foot will be on the lookout for her, and someone will question the neighbors. We'll do everything we can. I'm simply telling you that with girls this age, we usually find them within a couple of hours, a day at the most. They have almost always taken off on their own and returned on their own."

"So what am I supposed to do while you file your reports?"

"Well, there's a lot you can do, Mr. McKay. You can call your daughter's friends, ask them to call extended friends on the chance someone has seen her." It was obvious from his patience that he had given this speech to frantic parents before. "You could check out the beach and places she likes to hang out—the boardwalk, nearby arcades, the movies. I would suggest leaving Taylor's mother here to answer the phone."

Jarrett threw up his hands in frustration. "And when we don't find her in any of those places?"

"As I said, we'll do everything we can on our end. We'll find her." The officer offered a taut smile. "I understand your fears. I have a daughter of my own."

Maggie walked the officer to the door. "Thank you for coming, sir. We'll do all the things you suggested."

"You're welcome. I'll file the report and someone will be by with more questions."

"I can't believe this," Jarrett said angrily as Maggie closed the door behind the officer. "Someone has taken her, Maggie. I just know it."

Jarrett was a mess. He was still wearing last night's rumpled T-shirt and shorts, and he hadn't brushed his hair.

Maggie was just as frightened as Jarrett was, but if there was one thing her job as a physician had taught her, it was to appear calm even when she wasn't, to think logically, act on her logical thoughts, and fall apart later.

"Why don't you go change? Shave," she said gently. "You said Taylor has an address book in her room. I'll go through it and call everyone in it while you clean up."

He ran his hands through his hair. "I already called."

"That was hours ago." She faced him and rested both hands on his broad shoulders. She hated seeing him so scared and feeling so helpless. "Who knows? Maybe she's shown up somewhere by now."

Jarrett closed his eyes, then opened them again. "I'm not handling this well."

"You're handling this as well as any scared father could. Get cleaned up and you'll feel better."

He studied her face for a moment. "Thanks for being here, Maggie."

She tenderly brushed the hair off his forehead. Life was a hell of a roller-coaster ride. One minute she was lying in Jarrett's arms, on top of the world, and the next minute this. "She's my daughter, too. I'm scared, too."

"I know." He smiled grimly. "But I couldn't get through this without you. Not just because you're her mother, but because you're Maggie—the woman I love. The woman I've always loved."

His words filled her heart with joy, and yet she couldn't revel in that joy, because right now a part of both of them was missing.

They kissed like parents, like husband and wife. Like lovers.

"Go change now," she said gently, smoothing his stubbled cheek with her palm. "And I'll get on the phone." Maggie started down the hall behind him, giving him a pat on the shoulder. "Try not to worry. We'll find her. I know we will."

"Excuse me." Taylor knocked on the door after she heard Cal go up the steps. She was feeling calmer now. She was still afraid, terrified, but she knew she was going to be all right.

From what she gathered from the last conversation she'd heard, the one called Cal had somewhere to go, something about a phone call. She was hoping that meant he was calling her parents. It was already pretty obvious they hadn't kidnapped her to rape her or torture her or anything gross like that, so it had to be for ransom.

Cal had left Ants to guard her.

She knocked again. "Excuse me!"

"I'm not supposed to talk to you," Ants said.

Taylor could hear *Mr. Ed* on TV. The horse was talking, followed by a goofy laugh track.

"I'm hungry."

"Gave you a tuna fish sandwich and a Coke at lunch."

"I don't eat meat," she lied. The truth was, her stomach had been too queasy, but the kidnapper didn't have to know that. She had once seen a special on TV about kidnappings, and the man on the show had said that victims had the best chance of surviving if they made some kind of connection with the kidnappers, made them realize the victim was a real person. That's what she was doing, or at least trying to do. She had to do something or go crazy. "I'm a vegetarian," she called.

"A what?"

"I'm a vegetarian. I don't eat meat. I want a baked potato with broccoli and cheese."

"We ain't got no broccoli and potatoes here," Ants said, as if she'd just said something stupid. "Where you think I'm going to get that?"

"Arby's."

"We ain't got no Arby's around here. I'd have to go all the way into Talbany to go to Arby's. We ain't got nothing around here but a DQ and the gas station round the corner."

Taylor smiled. So they weren't in Talbany, and they weren't along the coast. If they were, there'd have been some fast-food place nearby. All the beach resorts had them. They must have gone west, out into the sticks. Somehow knowing where she was made her feel better.

"I'm awfully hungry," Taylor said, softening her

voice, trying to sound a little bit pitiful. If she could
get Ants to leave, she might be able to break down the
door and get out on her own. "Please, Ants? I'm *so*
hungry."

"I can't go nowhere." He paused. "I'm really sorry,"
he said then, "but you shouldn't be here too long."

"No? Why's that?" She stepped close to the door,
her hopes rising.

"I ain't supposed to talk to you."

"Come on. Tell me. I'm real scared, but if you tell
me I won't be."

"What the hell. What Cal won't know won't hurt
him." His hand met the door. "He done gone to call
your daddy. If your daddy drops off the money tomorrow morning like he's supposed to, you'll be out of
here before breakfast and we'll be on our way to
Vegas." He paused. "Shit," he cursed. "Don't tell Cal
I told you none of this."

Not until tomorrow morning, Taylor thought, tears
welling in her eyes. But she wanted to go home now.
Home to her father and Maggie. She wouldn't even
care if Maggie stayed the night. She just wanted to be
home safe.

Taylor laid her hand on the door. "Could my dad
pay now and I could go home now? I know he'll pay
as long as I'm not hurt," she said quickly.

"Yeah, that's what's Cal said. We saw his picture on
the cover of that there magazine at the mini-mart. Cal
said he had to be rich. Said he'd pay top dollar for his
daughter."

"He'd even pay more if you gave me back now."

"Nah, sorry. Cal says we got to let him stew overnight. That way there won't be no funny business in the morning over the money. He'll put it right where we tell him—no cops, no exploding ink shit."

Taylor glanced at the Porta-potty in the corner of the room. If she couldn't go home until tomorrow morning, she knew she'd have to use that disgusting thing.

She went back to the cot and flopped down on her back. She stared at the ceiling, trying to remain calm despite the tightening in her chest again. It sounded as if she was going to be OK. She knew her father would pay the ransom. She just had to hold out until morning.

She could do that. She knew she could, because she was tough, as tough as Maggie. Shoot, Maggie's husband and baby had gotten killed on the beltway and Maggie had survived it. Being kidnapped couldn't be near as bad as that. Taylor knew she'd just have to be brave, eat tuna, use the Porta-potty, and she'd be home for breakfast.

The phone rang at exactly four p.m., after Maggie had finished calling all Taylor's friends for the second time and Jarrett had just come into the house from driving up and down the beach avenue again.

Maggie and Jarrett's gazes met. The phone had been ringing all day, with Taylor's friends calling as well their concerned parents. Kyle had called, too. He was still out looking for Taylor.

Still, there was an instant of fear reflected in both their eyes. What if she'd drowned? What if she'd really been kidnapped? Or worse . . .

Maggie nodded to him. *Go ahead. Answer,* she was

saying. Her eyes were filled with concern and love not just for Taylor, but for him, too. Her love gave him the courage to answer the phone.

"Hello?"

"Mr. McKay?" The uneducated male voice sent a shiver of fear down Jarrett's spine.

He glanced up at Maggie, immediately getting her attention. "Yes, this is he."

"Mr. McKay, I'm going to give these instructions just once, so you listen," the man said. "You listen, and that little girl of yours will be just fine."

EIGHTEEN

Maggie exhaled as she sat on the edge of Jarrett's bed. The mattress gave as if it were as weary as she. All day she had been active making phone calls and driving up and down the avenue. Now there was nothing to do but wait, her energy spent.

Jarrett sat on the opposite edge, his back to her. Neither spoke. They were too tired, too stunned. Too scared.

Beyond the closed bedroom door, she could hear low voices in the living room. The FBI had been called in because of the ransom demand. They had camped out in the living room in case the kidnapper called again. The phone was tapped and a listening device had been attached to an extension. Right now the agents, two men and a woman, were drinking coffee and eating donuts Kyle had brought over before taking up residence in the kitchen.

The female agent, Jen Revel, had suggested Maggie and Jarrett get some sleep. Nine in the morning, the meeting time, would come soon enough.

Maggie had insisted Jarrett lie down, as well. He didn't have to sleep, she'd told him over his protests, but he would need to have his full wits about him tomorrow morning.

Maggie kicked off her sneakers and lay back, still in her white cotton work slacks and a pale blue T. She could smell their mingled scents on the pillow. The night they'd spent together seemed like a million years ago.

Jarrett's shoes hit the floor with a clump, clump, and he, too, lay back.

"Unbelievable," he mused aloud. "Some bastard has kidnapped my daughter."

"Jen says you were right, that spread in the magazine could very well have been what led the kidnappers to you."

He swore beneath his breath. "I knew I never should have let them print that article."

"Come on. You can't blame yourself. Information gets printed whether you want it to or not sometimes. I'm sure the magazine never thought anything like this would happen."

She paused. Jen had explained every step of the FBI's kidnapping-with-ransom procedure and made her feel much better about the whole situation. She wanted to pass on that same confidence to Jarrett. "Jen told me this guy is small time. It's obvious by the low sum of money he asked for. I mean, what's a hundred thousand dollars? She says he'll bungle it."

"Did she say my daughter would be all right?" His voice was thick, on the verge of tears.

Maggie rolled onto her elbow to face him. "She says in cases like this, they don't harm the victim. They just want the money."

Tears glistened in his eyes. "I don't know what I'll do if I lose her, Maggie. She's all I have."

"You're not going to lose her." For once, Maggie didn't tear up, although she ached at Jarrett's anguish. She brushed the blond hair from his eyes. "And she's not all you have. You have me."

He closed his eyes, seeming to try to get hold of himself, then opened them again. "Maggie, I know we're going to get her back. But if, God forbid if—" He teared up again. "If we lost her, would you . . ." He swore beneath his breath and glanced up at the ceiling fan, slowly turning.

"Would I what?" She closed her hand over his.

"I shouldn't even be thinking about this. Saying this." His voice cracked. "My daughter's gone and I'm worrying about myself."

She knew what he was trying to say and she understood his quandary. She had experienced the very same feelings when Stanley and Jordan had died. She had wondered how she could be so cold as to think of herself and her own feelings when her loved ones were dead. She knew now it was human nature, plain and simple, the instinct to survive in chaos.

"Are you asking me if I'll stick around without the daughter who brought me here?" She said it because he couldn't.

He nodded, his face taut with a mixture of emotions; fear, suffering, shame. "It's not right for me to ask. It's selfish and I—"

"We're not going to lose our daughter. But no matter what, I'll still be here," she whispered. She leaned over and kissed his forehead tenderly. "I'll be here if you'll have me, Jarrett."

Jarrett cupped the back of her head and urged her down to meet his lips. "God, I love you," he said fiercely. "And when this is over, when we have our daughter back, we're going to work this out, Maggie. I'll do anything to keep you both—to have you both, to have the three of us together like it should have been."

Tears slipped from her cheeks and fell on his. "You know how lucky we are?" she murmured. "To find each other again like this? To be given another chance?"

He smiled sadly, pulling her down to rest her head on his shoulder. "I know. Now let's try to get some sleep. We have to pick up our daughter in the morning."

"All right, Mr. McKay, do you understand our instructions?" Jen Revel, the FBI agent, spoke softly, but with an air of authority.

Jarrett was seated in the driver's seat of his car, a briefcase on the passenger's seat. As much as Maggie wanted to be in that seat, she knew she couldn't go. The kidnapper had said Jarrett and Jarrett alone. Maggie would follow behind him, just out of sight with Jen in an unmarked car.

"I understand," Jarrett said, upbeat. "I hand over the money, I take my daughter, and I get the hell out of the parking lot."

Jen nodded. "We come in. Block him off before he reaches the end of the street."

"Then you beat the crap out of him, I hope."

Jen laughed. "I'm afraid that's against the law, Mr. McKay, but I know the feeling." She squeezed his arm. "All right, sir, let's go. You've got four minutes."

Jen stepped away and Maggie crouched at Jarrett's door. "See you in five, with Taylor." She kissed him.

"See you in five." He flashed a smile.

It was forced, but Maggie would take what she could get right now. She backed away, and he closed his car door.

"Let's go, Maggie."

Maggie glanced up at the agent. She was tall, with a long blond ponytail. "I want you to let me out of this car just as soon as Jarrett has her."

"Just as soon as he's a safe distance," Jen assured her as they climbed into the small blue sedan.

Maggie's heart pounded as she slipped on her seat belt and watched Jarrett pull away. Jen let him get a full block down Ocean Highway before she followed him.

The meeting place was a mini-mart just off the main highway. Jarrett was to carry the briefcase to a dark blue van and exchange it for their daughter.

All Maggie could do now was pray fervently that nothing would go wrong, that Taylor was all right, that she and Jarrett would get away quickly.

"I see the van." Jarrett's voice came over the radio that lay on the seat between Jen and Maggie. He was wired, with a small microphone attached to the collar of his T-shirt so the agents could easily monitor the situation.

"Good," came a male voice. It was one of the other agents. "You know what to do. Please don't deviate from the plan, sir."

"I'm pulling into a parking slot with one space between us now," Jarrett said. He sounded calm, but Maggie recognized the stark fear in his voice. She could feel it, taste its bitterness on her tongue.

"Excellent," said the agent.

"It's not nine. Should I get out anyway?"

"Sure, Mr. McKay. Take the briefcase with you. Be sure to leave your motor running."

Maggie tightened her fists until her nails bit into the soft flesh of her palms. Jen pulled off on a side street a block away from the mini-mart. Maggie couldn't see what was happening from here. All of the police had to remain out of sight for Taylor's sake. Maggie could only hear what was happening.

"Here I go," Jarrett whispered.

Maggie heard the car door open.

There was a pause.

"I've got the money," Jarrett said stiffly. "I want to see my daughter."

"Lemme see the money," came a rougher, nervous voice.

"Let me see my daughter," Jarrett demanded forcefully.

Maggie held her breath.

She thought she heard the sound of another door opening. It squeaked like rusty metal.

"Taylor?" Jarrett said, his voice catching in his throat as if he was choking.

Jen reached over and squeezed Maggie's hand.

"Daddy."

Maggie covered her face. "Thank you," she whispered fervently. She felt as if a leaden weight had lifted from her chest. Taylor was safe! Her baby was safe!

"Take your damned money," Jarrett said.

The other man made a sound as if the air was knocked out of him. Had Jarrett thrown the briefcase at the kidnapper?

"Let's go home, sweetie," was the next phrase that came over the radio.

"OK, Daddy."

Taylor sounded shaken, but all right.

Again they heard the slam of a car door, almost simultaneously followed by the sound of squealing tires. "Taylor, climb over. Get into your belt," Jarrett urged frantically. "I've got her!"

Jarrett's old black BMW squealed around the corner. In the distance, police sirens howled.

Jarrett stopped the car in the middle of the street beside Jen's sedan. Maggie threw open the door of the unmarked car and ran for Jarrett's.

"Taylor!" Maggie yanked opened the passenger door and lunged inside, her arms widespread for her daughter.

Maggie felt Jarrett's hand on her shoulder as she took Taylor into her arms, seat belt and all. "I'm glad you're back safe, sweetie," Maggie managed around the lump in her throat. "And I love you, Taylor."

"Me, too," Taylor choked through her tears. "I love you, too, Mom."

"She asleep?"

Jarrett stood in the center of the living room and ran his fingers through his hair the way Maggie loved to watch him do. "Sound asleep. Light off. She's not in the least bit afraid. She says the kidnappers were too stupid to be frightening."

Maggie smiled. The police and FBI were gone and they were alone again. Of course there would be more interviews and then the trial, but it looked like a pretty tight case against the kidnappers. "She's tough," Maggie agreed. "Tough like her dad."

"Tough like her mom." He walked toward her. "I'd still like her to see that counselor Jen recommended, but I really think she's going to be all right. She says she knew we were coming for her, so she wasn't afraid."

Maggie put out her arms and looped them around his neck. The radio was playing softly from a cabinet missing one hinge—another of Jarrett's furniture assemblies that didn't go right.

Maggie and Jarrett slowly turned in a circle, their arms tight around each other.

"Don't know much about history. Don't know much biology," came the singer's melodious voice over the radio. It was an oldie but a goody.

"But I do know that I love you," Jarrett sang softly in her ear.

Maggie smiled, determined she wouldn't cry. She

wanted the tears to be over. She wanted a new life, another chance at happiness, and she knew that chance was right here in this house.

"Maggie?"

They still danced, slowly turning in a circle, just like when they were back in school. "Jarrett."

"Want to marry me?"

Her heart leaped in her breast, but she kept her tone casual, matching his. It was fun. A game. Things had been so serious for them since they'd been reunited that, somehow, this seemed right. "Sure."

"Tomorrow?"

She grimaced. "I have to work late. The next day?"

"No problem."

Their gazes met, followed by their lips. Maggie closed her eyes, reveling in the feel of his mouth against hers and his breath mingling with hers until it was one.

"I do love you," he whispered. "You know that?"

"I love you," she echoed.

He pulled back, catching her hands so he could look into her eyes again. "And you really will marry me?"

She was grinning, too. "I really will marry you."

"Then I have an engagement present for you."

Maggie crinkled her forehead. "A what?"

"An engagement present. Not a ring." He gestured. "But something just as good."

She laughed. "How can you have an engagement present? We just decided we were getting married a second ago."

"I've been saving it. Come on. You'll see." He

grabbed her hand and led her out the door, into the darkness and down the steps.

"Where are we going?" Maggie looked back up the steps. The deck light was on, illuminating the second-story living room balcony. "We can't leave Taylor."

"We're not leaving her. It's right here in the garage."

Maggie was utterly confused. She hadn't remembered there was a garage beneath the house.

Jarrett fished a pair of keys from his surf shorts and wiggled them in the old lock. It was a small garage, from outward appearances, barely large enough to fit a car.

"What are you doing?" Maggie laughed, enchanted. This was just like Jarrett, full of surprises. Always trying to make her smile.

He started to push up the door. "Close your eyes and let me get the light."

Maggie closed her eyes, becoming more and more curious. She heard the click of what sounded like an overhead light switch with a string pull. A second later he was beside her again.

"Ready?" He sounded like a little boy with a big surprise.

She laughed. "I'm ready already!"

"Look."

Maggie opened her eyes, then stared in shock. "Oh . . ." she breathed.

There, hidden in the tiny garage, was the '68 red Mustang convertible Jarrett had owned in high school. They'd shared their first kiss in this car. They'd fallen in love in this car. Sure, they'd just been kids, but the love had been real. Maggie knew that now.

"You kept it?" she breathed, still not sure she believed it really was the car.

"I didn't drive it after I came back from Spain," he confessed, emotion filling his voice. "I just couldn't, not without you."

"But you didn't sell it?"

"Couldn't bear to part with it, not even when I was short on cash back when Taylor was a baby. I guess somewhere in my subconscious I always knew you'd forgive me. You'd come back."

Maggie stepped toward the convertible and brushed her hand along the smooth, red hood. The cool metal sent a shiver through her as memories of the past flooded her—the recollection of what it had felt like to be in love for the first time, the thrill of riding with the top down, the wind in her hair, Jarrett at her side.

"Get in," he urged.

She started for the passenger side.

"No, the driver's seat."

She glanced up. "But that's not how it was. I never drove your car."

He tossed her the key, already pulling open the passenger door. "No, that wasn't how it was, but things are going to be different this time, aren't they?"

Maggie walked around, opened the door, and slid in. "Yes," she said, unable to stop smiling. "They're going to be different. Better. Now that we have Taylor."

"Now that we're older, and hopefully a little smarter about things." He winked.

Maggie rested her hands on the steering wheel for a moment, breathing in the scent of the leather upholstery he had kept clean all these years. Then, meeting his gaze, she leaned over the seat. His lips met hers. This time she wasn't flooded by old memories, but imagined the new ones they would make together.

EPILOGUE

Twelve Years Later

The phone rang, awakening Maggie from a deep sleep. She reached for it even before she opened her eyes. After all these years of being a physician, even now that she rarely was on call, she was instantly alert. "Dr. Turner."

"Mom?"

Maggie sat up on the edge of the bed and flipped on the bedside lamp. "Taylor?" she said anxiously. She glanced at the clock; it was almost two a.m.

Behind her, sprawled out on the bed asleep, Jarrett muttered something about phone calls in the middle of the night.

Maggie sensed the tightness in her daughter's voice. "What is it, Taylor?"

"Mom, I need you. John's on his way home from that business trip, but his flight doesn't arrive for another two hours. Then he's got to drive home from the airport."

Maggie climbed out of bed, naked, and searched for her clothes on the floor. It had been hers and Jarrett's anniversary yesterday. They had shared wine on the beach last night, built a sandcastle, made love on the living room floor, then here in the bed. The room was a mess.

"What's the matter, Taylor?" Cradling the phone on her shoulder, she grabbed a pair of jeans and hopped on one foot to slip into them.

"It's the baby, Mom. I'm in labor."

"OK," Maggie spoke calmly, though her heart pounded. This was her baby. *Her* baby was having a baby. "You're sure?"

"Mom . . ."

Maggie smiled. She knew that tone well, that *Mom, I'm not stupid* tone. She grabbed the corner of the pillow Jarrett was wrapped around and tugged. "Jarrett, wake up. The baby's coming."

Jarrett mumbled in his sleep and rolled over onto his side, away from her.

"OK," Maggie said into the phone. "I can be there in half an hour. Is that soon enough, or do you think you need an ambulance?"

"Mom, it's just a baby. A first baby, at that. I think I have the half hour."

Maggie laughed. Taylor had the same calm logic she had. Taylor never got flustered. "Do you want me to bring your dad?"

It was Taylor's turn to laugh. "Yeah, right, as if he's going to be of any help in labor and delivery. No, Mom, let him sleep. Tell him to come to the hospital in the morning. Then leave him a note, because in the morning he won't remember anyway."

Maggie grabbed a white T-shirt off the floor. It was

Jarrett's, but she pulled it on anyway. She took the phone from her ear just long enough to pop her head through the neck. "Anything you need?"

She knew Taylor was smiling. She could hear it in her voice.

"Just you, Mom."

"See you in half an hour."

"See you. I'll be packed and ready to go."

Maggie hung up the phone and padded barefoot to the bathroom to grab a hairbrush. She glanced at her reflection in the mirror and was surprised by the tears that welled in her eyes.

The day she had married Jarrett, she had known her life with him and their daughter would be good, but she had never fathomed it would be this good. She had never imagined after all the pain of her younger years that she could be this happy, this content, never imagined her relationship with her daughter would bloom into a cherished friendship in Taylor's adult years. For the last twelve years, Jarrett and Taylor had been her world. Though they could never replace her little Jordan, they had dulled that pain of loss until it was nothing but an occasional ache. Jarrett's love had healed her wounds.

And now Taylor was going to have a baby. She and Jarrett were going to be grandparents. Against all odds, there would be another baby for Maggie to love.

ABOUT THE AUTHOR

Colleen Faulkner lives with her family in southern Delaware and is the daughter of the best-selling historical romance author Judith French. Colleen is the author of twenty Zebra historical romances and is currently working on a contemporary romance trilogy for Zebra's Bouquet line called *Bachelors Inc.* The first title, *Marrying Owen,* will be published August, 2000. She loves to hear from readers, and you may write to her c/o Zebra books. Please include a self-addressed stamped envelope if you wish a response.

BOOK YOUR PLACE ON OUR WEBSITE AND MAKE THE READING CONNECTION!

We've created a customized website just for our very special readers, where you can get the inside scoop on everything that's going on with Zebra, Pinnacle and Kensington books.

When you come online, you'll have the exciting opportunity to:

- View covers of upcoming books
- Read sample chapters
- Learn about our future publishing schedule (listed by publication month *and author*)
- Find out when your favorite authors will be visiting a city near you
- Search for and order backlist books from our online catalog
- Check out author bios and background information
- Send e-mail to your favorite authors
- Meet the Kensington staff online
- Join us in weekly chats with authors, readers and other guests
- Get writing guidelines
- AND MUCH MORE!

**Visit our website at
http://www.zebrabooks.com**

COMING IN MARCH FROM
ZEBRA BOUQUET ROMANCES

#37 LOVE ON THE RUN by Leigh Greenwood
__(0-8217-6531-0, $3.99) Accused of selling company secrets to the competition, investment banker Claire Dalton is desperate to stay out of jail. Eric Sterling doubts her innocence—until a savage attack convinces him that someone wants her dead. Now, his need to protect her stirs up passionate desires he finds hard to control.

#38 LITTLE WHITE LIES by Judy Gill
__(0-8217-6532-9, $3.99) Doug Fountain needs a fiancée—for a month only. That will be enough time for his grandfather to hand over the family business to a "suitable heir." Doug hopes to find a woman who will go along with his scheme . . . if he promises her the right deal. And that deal definitely doesn't include love—or does it?

#39 LOOKING FOR PERFECTION by Valerie Kirkwood
__(0-8217-6533-7, $3.99) From the moment Mitch Ballard meets high-spirited Zoe, there are downright fireworks. But his life is complicated enough right now, and the last thing he needs is to tumble head over heels in love. If only his heart didn't find her so absolutely irresistible!

#40 THE LAST TRUE COWBOY by Mary Schramski
__(0-8217-6534-5, $3.99) A heartbreaking marriage to a bull rider taught Beth Morris the hard way that family comes last for thrill-seeking men. So when handsome rider Trace Barlow shows up at her ranch, she has no intention of giving this reckless cowboy the time of day. Can Trace convince Beth that the only prize he's interested in winning is her heart?

Put a Little Romance in Your Life With
Fern Michaels

__Dear Emily   0-8217-5676-1 $6.99US/$8.50CAN

__Sara's Song   0-8217-5856-X $6.99US/$8.50CAN

__Wish List   0-8217-5228-6 $6.99US/$7.99CAN

__Vegas Rich   0-8217-5594-3 $6.99US/$8.50CAN

__Vegas Heat   0-8217-5758-X $6.99US/$8.50CAN

__Vegas Sunrise   1-55817-5983-3 $6.99US/$8.50CAN

__Whitefire   0-8217-5638-9 $6.99US/$8.50CAN

Call toll free **1-888-345-BOOK** to order by phone or use this coupon to order by mail.

Name_____
Address_____
City _____ State _____Zip_____
Please send me the books I have checked above.
I am enclosing $_____
Plus postage and handling* $_____
Sales tax (in New York and Tennessee) $_____
Total amount enclosed $_____
*Add $2.50 for the first book and $.50 for each additional book.
Send check or money order (no cash or CODs) to:
Kensington Publishing Corp., 850 Third Avenue, New York, NY 10022
Prices and Numbers subject to change without notice.
All orders subject to availability.
Check out our website at **www.kensingtonbooks.com**

Celebrate Romance With Two of Today's Hottest Authors

Meagan McKinney

__In the Dark	$6.99US/$8.99CAN	0-8217-6341-5
__The Fortune Hunter	$6.50US/$8.00CAN	0-8217-6037-8
__Gentle from the Night	$5.99US/$7.50CAN	0-8217-5803-9
__A Man to Slay Dragons	$5.99US/$6.99CAN	0-8217-5345-2
__My Wicked Enchantress	$5.99US/$7.50CAN	0-8217-5661-3
__No Choice But Surrender	$5.99US/$7.50CAN	0-8217-5859-4

Meryl Sawyer

__Thunder Island	$6.99US/$8.99CAN	0-8217-6378-4
__Half Moon Bay	$6.50US/$8.00CAN	0-8217-6144-7
__The Hideaway	$5.99US/$7.50CAN	0-8217-5780-6
__Tempting Fate	$6.50US/$8.00CAN	0-8217-5858-6
__Unforgettable	$6.50US/$8.00CAN	0-8217-5564-1

Call toll free **1-888-345-BOOK** to order by phone, use this coupon to order by mail, or order online at www.kensingtonbooks.com.

Name _____

Address _____

City _____ State _____ Zip _____

Please send me the books I have checked above.

I am enclosing	$_____
Plus postage and handling*	$_____
Sales tax (in New York and Tennessee only)	$_____
Total amount enclosed	$_____

*Add $2.50 for the first book and $.50 for each additional book.

Send check or money order (no cash or CODs) to:

Kensington Publishing Corp., Dept. C.O., 850 Third Avenue, New York, NY 10022

Prices and numbers subject to change without notice.

All orders subject to availability.

Visit our website at **www.kensingtonbooks.com.**

**LOVE STORIES YOU'LL NEVER FORGET . . .
IN ONE FABULOUSLY ROMANTIC NEW LINE**

BALLAD ROMANCES

Each month, four new historical series by both beloved and brand-new authors will begin or continue. These linked stories will introduce proud families, reveal ancient promises, and take us down the path to true love. In Ballad, the romance doesn't end with just one book . . .

*COMING IN JULY
EVERYWHERE BOOKS ARE SOLD*

The Wishing Well Trilogy:
CATHERINE'S WISH, by Joy Reed.
When a woman looks into the wishing well at Honeywell House, she sees the face of the man she will marry.

Titled Texans:
NOBILITY RANCH, by Cynthia Sterling
The three sons of an English earl come to Texas in the 1880s to find their fortunes . . . and lose their hearts.

Irish Blessing:
REILLY'S LAW, by Elizabeth Keys
For an Irish family of shipbuilders, an ancient gift allows them to "see" their perfect mate.

The Acadians:
EMILIE, by Cherie Claire
The daughters of an Acadian exile struggle for new lives in 18th-century Louisiana.